CENTRAL

c1

Dawson, Fielding, 1930-
    A great day for a ballgame; a conscious
love story.   Bobbs-Merrill [c1973]

    I. Title

A
Great
Day
for a
Ballgame

Other Books by Fielding Dawson

AN EMOTIONAL MEMOIR OF FRANZ KLINE

KRAZY KAT / THE UNVEILING

OPEN ROAD

THE BLACK MOUNTAIN BOOK

THE DREAM / THUNDER ROAD

THE MANDALAY DREAM

THE GREATEST STORY EVER TOLD

THE SUN RISES INTO THE SKY

A
GREAT
DAY
FOR A
BALLGAME
A

Conscious

Love

Story

by

Fielding

Dawson

clc

THE BOBBS-MERRILL COMPANY, INC.

INDIANAPOLIS   NEW YORK

The Bobbs-Merrill Company, Inc.
Publishers   Indianapolis   New York
Copyright © 1973 by Fielding Dawson
All rights reserved
ISBN 0–672–51794–9
Library of Congress Catalogue card number 72–9880
Printed in the United States of America
Designed by Jack Jaget

For My Sister, Cara
and The Good Life

'It's a great day for a ballgame.'

—ERNIE BANKS

The Kinetic Line, 1944

'I made no remark,' he said.
'Remarks want you to make them,' I said.

—RAYMOND CHANDLER
Farewell, My Lovely

The small yellow Piper Cub airplane made a long right bank against the blue Midwestern sky; my sister was up there, learning how to fly with the CAP instructor, and as I stood on the concrete landing strip in front of the hangar, looking up at the plane, it was also as if I were above it, gazing down at it flying over the farms and lakes and me too, down there below, so the plane seemed fixed, like a lazy fly in my—what's the word—Consciousness.

Yes. The small airport was in southern Illinois, near Horse Shoe Lake, and was owned by Mrs. Sam Breadon, and Sam owned the St. Louis Cardinals. So it was altogether a day to fly, and to respond to where my sister was, and the plane—which I did, later that day; he took me up, and let me fly it, a little—a day for the touch of the controls, a day for the future, and like in déjà vue, it seemed that me and consciousness and the day touched each other passing along and therefore, to me personally, in my short pants, watching the yellow plane in the sky, it was a *great* day for a ballgame.

1969
New York
The Kinetic Line
Becomes
the Storyline:

I woke suddenly, and intuitively glanced at the tide, got out of bed fast, talking to myself while I shaved and dressed automatically sorting through the papers on my desk in my office in the job in my head, and as I put on my tie I finished the letter to the fellow in Suffolk County reminding him of the COD fee the dispatcher Cerar at Sternberger Trucking had quoted me, and in back of that in my mind I began the claim against the New England Trucking firm St. Johnsbury about the Fitzgerald delivery, and I also completed the preparation of two refunds which would keep my company out of small-claims court, and as I stopped at my studio/loft door, as I always do—for a last look around—I saw my typewriter in a flash of wish and anger at the stack of blank white paper ready beside it, and the sheet in the machine half-filled with words *I felt tears, and a terrible sadness.*

My sister said,

You remember the old streetcar conductor on the rides we took to Washington University at night?

I said sure, and remembered the two of us—one night a week—taking the wonderful old 01 Streetcar ride to the university's art department where she was sculpting a head of me—I loved the smell of clay in the classroom—but the streetcar rides were so filled with feeling, and I think

*of the war years, night, ice cream, snow and my sister and
I—*

*He was the conductor of the streetcar that hit and
nearly killed you. It was the year before he would have
retired, and he was heartbroken when he saw it was you.
He remembered us. He remembered you.*

What a sweet old man he was. So kind and warm to
us and I saw the brand-new first-draft manuscript to the
right of my typewriter with the glass paperweight on it
that mother had given to my wife as a wedding present,
and when my wife and I split up it got left behind, a blue
and crimson abstract fire flower, to remind me of her
power as in a gesture; I leaned across my desk and read
the dust jacket of my new book, tacked on the wall; the
publisher had sent it to me, with a note so typical of him,
patience my lad, *the book will out!*

I went down the steps, my mind busy over all the ac-
tivities of a new love book being written, and one just
finished about how Kipling had saved my life in Missouri
—plus a collection of short stories being published on the
West Coast and as I glanced into my mailbox on the way
out, I saw a couple of letters, and put them in my pocket
and left my building walking rapidly down Park Avenue
South, crossing eastward on Union Square North (17th
Street), and heading staircase fashion down across town
to lower Fifth Avenue, and as I walked, it slowly dawned
on me that the envelope of one of the letters was of special seeming significance, and I took it out and saw the
name of the international and very famous fashion magazine in the upper lefthand corner, and the address, and
as I walked downtown on Fifth—the other letter was
from Fred, surely patiently saying he and Bea would love
to see me, would I call them? I promised myself I would,
guiltily, and opened the other envelope and took out the
letter, very crisp light-blue paper with a dark-blue letter-
head and a warm, businesslike message that set my heart
pounding. I crossed 14th Street and read my own name

and address, and with a paragraph indent: Dear Mr. Dawson, it said; the editor was proud to accept my story, they had been trying to phone me but couldn't get me, and if I would accept the admittedly low payment of $175.00 they hoped to have it in the August issue, and would I call them and arrange a date we could get together and discuss it? Her signature was small, neat and businesslike, yet shy and strong, and having opened the door to my office, and saying hello to John and Jacques, who worked with me, I opened the container of coffee at my desk, added sugar and sipped, and laughed hey hey hey

'Play ball!' I cried, and called the magazine.

I asked a bright young voice if I could speak to Mrs. West, and the voice said you mean the literary department, and I said yes and she said in a yep just a moment song and I waited and a warm young woman's voice said Yes?

I asked for Mrs. West and the voice inquired who was calling and I told her and she said Oh Mr. Dawson, we really love your story, really, would you hold? I'll put you through to Mrs. West, and then I heard a stillness and then a woman's voice, very soft but professionally charming, oh wow there, I thought—'Hi, Mr. Dawson!'

'Hi,' I laughed.

'You got my letter?'

'I did; and thank you.'

'Well,' she said, shifting papers on her desk, 'we're a little humiliated by the money bit, but it's all they'll give us—sorry: please understand.'

'Yes sure.'

'I can try for more, but don't plan on it, and what I'd like to—'

'I won't.'

'Good, is to get you on the cover.'

'You won't; they only mention the merchandise.'

She laughed. 'Still, I'll try. Want to come up and sign the contract and have lunch?'

There was a quality of stimulation in her voice that pleased me in a way I could only call proper—happy; as if she too, was, but then maybe it was she just wanted an excuse to do something different—kick the boredom—get out of the office, etc., oh yeah? And maybe not! Maybe she wanted to meet me, maybe she was curious. She took the story, didn't she?

She did indeed.

So we set up a date.

I stood at the foot of the skyscraper where the sun played rainbow games with a water fountain, and young couples ate their lunches on the edges of the pool. What a neighborhood. Tiffany's, the Museum of Modern Art, Bergdorf's, and the Plaza. Fifth Avenue traffic slanted noisily along behind me.

I looked up.

A lady editor was behind a desk in the sky, waiting, and my own curiosity, like a spark, hung beside my left temple as I walked through the lobby; my eyes caught the correct floor on the glassed-in directory, and me and my unconscious went flying up together, and as I got off and walked along the marble corridor, neither a threatening marble corridor, nor a romantic one: marble, steel, glass, the prototype of the model business museum; I felt a little like on display.

The glass doors ahead of me enhanced—and even named—the image I pushed into, and I walked toward the young receptionist who, with fixed smile, asked me my name, and the smile stayed still when I told her, and she spoke into a powder-blue telephone that Mr. Dawson was here: in soft tones, having been in a storyline, and a younger woman, in fact almost a girl, very slim and pretty, came around a corner, and walked toward me. We shook hands, and introduced ourselves, she was the assistant literary editor, she said, and as we walked down the corridor passing editorial offices, she complimented me on my story. I said,

'The last tide I was here, this place wasn't. It was in a different part of town. Right?'

'It sure was,' she laughed. Nice warm walk.

'On Madison, wasn't it?'

'Yes,' she said. 'But that *was* a tide ago, wasn't it!'

I nodded; eager ego: 'They had the art department flush against the literary department, with cubbyhole-partitioned offices. Mazelike.'

'Wasn't Dale editor then?'

'Yes,' I said, and felt a little guilty; mazelike wasn't the word, and Dale had seemed anything but a man in a maze. But had he been? What was the word, and who— or what—was mazelike?

Disorganized. You were the maze. Still are.

We turned a corner, me nodding yes to myself, and she tapped on a cream-colored steel door; a voice said come in, and she went in, and said, 'Amelia, this is Mr. Dawson;' she stepped aside to let me pass and said to me, 'This is our Literary Editor, Amelia West.' I felt there was a little chill between them, and I stepped in looking out the window behind Amelia West, seeing the borough of Queens, smoking beyond the East River; the Triborough Bridge arched across like a piece in the puzzle of Manhattan's constant attempt to be the city in Rimbaud's *Illuminations;* and then I saw black pupils centered in October gray irises, a pair of level crescent eyes above a tightlipped smile which broke into a grin as we shook hands as she—but she had appeared before me, she was standing before me as I heard the door close with a motion which if it didn't exit the assistant editor, it helped, and the door was closed before I could thank her assistant, and then we were alone, I was a little baffled and Mrs. West was saying how much she enjoyed the story, but that well a couple of changes had to be made, and with the ease, in the storyline suddenly my manuscript was before me, the page was open to a red mark her left hand indicated, as I took off my scarf and raincoat, I heard her say oh—and as she extracted a filter cigarette from a box, my coat and scarf were hanging on a coatrack in the corner, there was no ring on her left hand, and as my lips parted in amazement, she said,

'We have to change this. Can we say, ah . . . screw?'

I looked at my coat on the rack and murmured you sure work fast, and said, 'Sure. Cut fuck.'

She looked at me and I looked at her and she tilted her head, smiled to me (a wiseguy), and gestured well, yes, as I dug in my pocket for a match and two of my French cigarettes, 'We,' she chuckled, 'that is, they, you know the They?'

Do I know the They. 'I know the They. Would you like one of these?'

'Still think fuck is dirty, oh *yes*, thanks,' and she put her filter cigarette on her desk, took one of mine and I lit both and then she was at my side puffing, talking about page twelve, saying, *she was saying, do you mean that,*

'Do you mean that reversal of the adjective—it's part of your style, I know—but they're confused by it.'

Pretty tricky Fielding. I nodded, and indicating the sentence, 'And she was of love; and pretty, Fielding,' I read, and told her, 'Between you and me I didn't know how to get ahead with it, so I thought if I used the adjective there it would give it a leap,' and I paused, in my own storyline. 'I think it must be there,' I said, 'but maybe move it around—in fact try it.'

She did. She wrote, as I said, 'And she was pretty, and of love; Fielding,' and I laughed, and said to Amelia West, 'Yrs truly,' as she erased it and returned it to the original, murmuring you use the first person personal Fielding, that's good, and I said,

'It's still a gambit, not a gimmick.'

'Yes, the feminine becomes you—you might be self-conscious about it, particularly in your newer work—no, this is yours, it belongs to you.'

I said, 'Wait a second—how can you be so—'

She went on, a little triumphantly, and a dash of arrogance: 'All right, look at that sentence. Name another writer who could write that—or who would think to.'

I read the sentence and nodded. 'Yes,' I admitted. 'It's good.'

'And original.' She pointed out a few punctuation and spelling mistakes she had corrected and then she got the contract and put it on the desk in front of me, and explained it; an elementary one-page contract wherein they get the first serial rights, the copyright, and that I won't sell it to anybody else until thirty days after publication; a neat job, I thought, for $175.00, and I signed two copies and kept one, she put the other in a manila folder and gestured to a chair, and we both sat down, she saying I had been right.

'About that contract?' I asked.

'No,' she laughed. She knew. 'The cover. We can't mention you on the cover, and although I had hoped we could feature your story, we can't. I'm sorry. Because of the fashions and ads we have so little space allowed us—and they might, they might even ask you to cut it. God.'

'It's all right,' I said, and felt the reverse—anger at my story nesting in with the Tampax, falsies, and lipstick. She laughed, reading me, there was something from a very ancient world in this woman, and as she put out her cigarette she looked at me.

'We thought August, but the new date is July—but.'

'I'll wire mother September,' I smiled. 'Do you enjoy the view?'

She made a little smile, but didn't turn. I looked at her, and for some reason felt her tense, yet just then, with a sudden subtle change, her face brightened; and she looked fake, like me, and she said they'd found a good artist to do the illustration. Stick to the point, i.e.

Was it a warning? Had I disappointed her? 'Is he going to do the Kat?' I asked.

'We don't know, yet,' she said, and her face paled, slightly, and then color returned as she mentioned the artist's name; I hadn't heard of him, and she said she'd call me and let me see what he submitted. Detective story. She was responding, but to what? She was nervous. I stood up, put out my cigarette, I smoke them below the dead line, and she stood up, and suddenly my coat and scarf were in her hands—'Wait!' I cried—'do that again.'

She looked surprised. 'Do what again?'

'That,' I said. 'How did you get my coat and scarf from there to here without me seeing you.'

She frowned square in my face. 'I don't understand.'

'I didn't see you do, what, you—oh fu—screw it,' I laughed. 'It must be me.'

Remembering the vanishing assistant editor and the closed door, and realizing when I mentioned the view it reminded Amelia West that she was in a little room in a skyscraper office building, and I felt someone near me, a sister of sorts, and childhood, *if I could only keep my big mouth shut.*

She helped me into my coat with a subtle smile, took a hint of a first motion toward the coatrack, an old fashioned thing, and I said,

'Stop.'

She stopped.

I went to the coatrack, took her coat off, and leisurely helped her into it, and I looked at her, wanting to explain I couldn't take another one of her mystic transporting tricks.

'Where'd you get the coatrack?' I asked, instead.

'In an antique store. I want a drink. Hungry?'

'Yes twice, first most.' And I looked around her office. The walls were bare. Not even a calendar. A psychedelic or Black Power poster or—most important—a mirror. She must hate the place.

She walked toward the door, and opened it, and as we went into the corridor she said, softly,

'I don't like it here.'

Looking down at her upturned intuitive face I saw the line her lips made, a very soft storyline that almost invisibly trembled between her lower lip and her chin, the little blur in the sudden glance up at me, and we were walking along the corridor, me thinking the reason she had paled was because once again I had—me and my ego—had barged in and started noticing the things; with a little thought I could have known she hated the view.

'I'll write the bio notes,' she said. 'Do you have a photograph we can use?'

'I can get one. Anything else you need?'

We passed the reception desk, I smiled at the woman there, and held the glass door, and Amelia West and I went out into the vacant marble display corridor. It seemed to wait for bodies, and as she poked the elevator button, she said,

'No, I know about you.'

'You do?'

'Sure. I read your last book. I thought it was *great*. I can go from there; they won't give me but a line or two, anyway.'

We leaned against the wall, and she said, almost grimly,

'They might, just might, ask you to cut it. I'll let you know.'

'Don't lose sleep,' I smiled. But I was angry. 'Let's wait and see,' I said, coolly. She nodded the same.

The elevator came, in fact I almost fell into it, she reached out and grabbed me, I kept on my feet, though, and recovered, and she buttoned her coat, murmured, 'Good, thanks, I'm glad you said that,' and she jammed her hands into her pockets.

Down we flew.

Out, walking through the lobby and shoved the door open and were into the street. We crossed Fifth Avenue and walked briskly uptown, she saying she knew of a good French restaurant, and me like a tall man in a dirty cream-colored raincoat smiling at the city, and Amelia West, success with not much money, my typical luck, and on my lips and taste buds, the tingling a priori taste, of a delicious ice-cold vodka martini.

The crosstown street was in a pandemo-
nium of jackhammer racket and screaming street repair and
we timidly stepped around sawhorses, edged between dump
trucks and cement mixers, I helped her across a smashed-up
sidewalk, the noise was deafening and the door to the
French restaurant opened and a Large Black Man pushed
a wheelbarrow piled full of fractured plaster across our
path, one of the waiters greeted her saying in French they
were closed for repairs. Her face fell.

'But this is the only place I come to! I like it—'

The waiter shrugged as she—angrily—laughed. Should
I even mention it.

She thought, and we walked, as on thin ice, out onto
what was or had been, the sidewalk, and I said look there's
a place up ahead, and a moment later we looked in to a
not altogether friendly doorway and then at each other.

'I see another,' I said. And in a peculiar way, I realized
my right fist could feel sudden, that I was angry for her, and
wanted it to work. So I felt strong. Storyline.

We walked toward Sixth Avenue and looked into a
cartoon friendly doorway, went in and as the waiter approached us with his eyebrows up and his fingers in the V
which means peace these days, I nodded with true force, I
had been in the Army, and he hustled away and was waiting for us by a table for two nicely spaced away from the

18

lunch crowd but near enough to the bar action, in a kind of alcove, it was, like, and we could just see the front window looking out onto the devastated street scene, and she seemed really pleased. I helped her with her coat, held a chair as she glissandoed in and I took off my coat and sat down, looked at her, even to her storyline, not—

'Whiskey sour not too sour,' she said to me, her eyes on the waiter.

'Whiskey sour not too sour, and a martini, vodka, very very dry on the rocks with a twist and a club soda chaser.'

'Very good,' he said softly. 'Will you have lunch?'

We nodded. 'But not yet.' And I laughed, suddenly; for some reason I felt release, and it felt comic. She was looking at me.

May I have another one of your cigarettes?'

'Sure.' Our eyes met.

I offered her one, and lit it for her and as I put the pack on the table she sat back, puffing. I bit my lip and said,

'I'm just about broke. Do you have an expense account?'

'Oh hell yes!' she laughed gaily. 'Thank God!'

'Well,' I said, 'Wednesdays are tough.' What's that?

'Thursday is payday,' she smiled. I did a small double-take, and thought a moment. Yes, it was true, and I asked,

'Why don't you like it back there?'

She said, 'All those anxious people, and their fashion world.'

'And you, lost in it, and probably angry,' Who? Guess.

Ha. She smiled and whispered, 'Yeah,' glanced at me, 'let's talk about you.'

Level crescent eyes, and I saw the secret sensitive intelligence lines. I looked out the front window.

'Come on,' she said.

I looked at her and made a movie-star smile. 'Come on?'

'Yes,' she said directly, and her lips moved in a different smile. 'Come on.'

She looked at me as if I was missing something, and she said,

'You don't know what come on means?'

'You're asking me if I don't know what come on means? Are you coming on?'

She really laughed, and murmured probably, and the waiter angled our drinks down before us. He opened a small bottle of club soda and poured it over a glass of ice. We raised our drinks as I thanked him, and as he went away, with the smile signifying a coupla wiseguys in the corner—meaning *me*; and then Amelia West.

'To you,' I said.

'To you,' she smiled.

I looked at her and she looked at me. 'To us, then; a party.'

'Ah,' she warmly said, 'that's nice,' and in a kind of power, again I felt the past. But.

'Good martini! Um *boy*,' and I sipped. 'Perfect. Yours?'

'Yes, very good. Fresh orange juice.'

I lit a cigarette. 'Amazing the difference. How was the tiger hunt?'

'Quite good!' she nodded. 'Drink much?'

'Too much. Why don't you like your job—deeper reason.'

'Why?'

I blinked. 'Yes. Why. But what do you mean why— why'd I ask? I mean I like to drink, it keeps me involved with myself.'

'You couldn't mean that, and anyway what's too much?'

You, I thought. 'I do mean it. How can you say that; in fact, what's happening? I have—no. I tend toward chaos; I lose sight of myself, am more than one man, and that's my storyline.'

I laughed. She said,

'You're self-conscious—of what. Tell me.'

'Yes. In fact, very well said. In fact, wow. And please—'

She sipped her drink and sighed. I relit my cigarette and my hand shook. I puffed. I was just a little startled, as she said,

'As rationalizations go, it's not bad. At least you've got one.' And she added, 'Do you do this often?'

'Do what.' Often. No. And as I see you, never. It happened only once. She smiled and I had a regressive twinge; the cue? Had I missed another one? Damn! cried the baby. 'No,' I laughed. 'Do you?'

'No,' she said. 'But I'm surprised. You're a known writer, no?'

'No,' I laughed and laughed to her, 'that is, except—'

Luckily I let it hang, because I didn't like the way her head had turned away, and then she looked fully at me. 'Sure you are. And you're the most self-conscious person I've ever met.'

I looked at her not knowing whether she liked it or not, but her long sentence confirmed something, that out of my past—just as I was feeling her past, or the presence of her past—her cards, sticks, marbles, chips, numbers and goofy combinations, she played decisively, and the warmth in her voice was the warmth of her response to it, and she was warmly insisting I relax and enjoy it. Literally.

I said, 'To you, you—'

She looked startled. 'Sure! But to others, too.' There was just a touch of plea.

'Listen,' I said, 'fame is—I don't know what fame is, except that it's very dangerous, and what I do is get up in the morning, go to work, and afterwards go to the bar, have a few and go home.'

'And write? What do you do—at your job.'

'Don't rub it in,' I said unfairly, but angry. 'I'm the service manager for a furniture store.' Boy.

'But why?' She was honest.

'Do you think I live off my writing?'

'Why aren't you an editor, why aren't you in publishing?'

'Because I hate it,' I said levelly. 'Just like you.'

She didn't say anything and she had a look in her eyes as though she were standing on a high hill, under a blue sky, on a summer afternoon and about to persuade God to take some hard action on the New York publishing world. 'Mmm,' she said, sipping.

I put out the dead cigarette, and sat back in my chair. The restaurant was just dark blue enough, and looking at her, I wondered if it was the martini in me, she was very handsome, and with style; a shy, for some reason courageous identity came out of her and hovered around her, but, she was frightened. We both were. Yet determined, and decisive, and suddenly I liked her. I sipped my drink. Like me. She said,

'Why do you hate it.' *Don't look at me like that*.

I leaned forward saying, 'You're very perceptive. You know. It's a speech, but publishing isn't for me. I like to be independent with my writing, and, in a paradox, because I would love to be an editor because I would do it right, i.e., respect the writer, but every experience I've had with publishing, editors, book and magazine publication, and even teaching causes me to get overinvolved. Much too much.'

'Yet you said you hated it.'

'Yes. Remember; think of the shit they publish. I couldn't edit that, or work with editors that do.'

She stepped into the pitch: 'Don't you like editors?'

'No.'

She smiled, finished her drink and put out the cigarette. 'Another?'

'Definitely,' and I finished mine. I signaled the waiter and felt in a good mood, suddenly. I sipped a little club soda, and said up to him,

'Two more, please, and keep 'em like they was.'

He made a fake smile and disappeared. I said,

'I feel sentimental.'

'With all your hatred of editors, you? Sentimental?'

'You know what editors I mean. And sure, I'm a sentimental guy.'

'You are?'

'Mm hum, anything the matter with a sentimental guy?'

'Nooo, or at least—'

'No? or at least not if you like him, right?'

'Right,' she smiled.

'Do you ever have the feeling the person you're talking with is your own voice?'

'No.'

'No—?'

'No. But you do.'

'Yes. That's the storyline.'

Her face darkened into a whole scowl. 'I don't,' she said evenly, 'understand that.'

I said, 'Dialogue. I feel my voice following within me, and I listen, as in that inexplicable first feel that déjà vue is about to happen. I had the sensation then, that what you said or asked about my being sentimental was my voice, speaking to me.'

'I don't feel that,' she said. 'And other things.'

'O.K. and sorry, I don't mean to steal you from yourself, yet the world is also subtle, and when you teased me about being sentimental, I thought it was that I was a sentimental guy, but you meant to be, to be sentimental, and your real humor was that I was going around in circles about being a sentimental guy, when everyone else is going around in circles about being, being sentimental.'

'True; and I apologize. What's the storyline?'

'Pure energy. Us. The dialogue of response.'

'And?'

'Like this.'

'What. Please, Fielding.'

'What—to what, to us.'

'I'm lost. I think,' she grinned.

'O.K. I'll tell you a story. When I was in college there was a girl and we were very close, and we used to play games, we used to play being each other, and she'd speak to me like me, and I'd speak to her like her. We were responding to each other so fully we turned into each other, she would speak to me as she spoke to herself, and I likewise to me to her, and the real fun was when I turned feminine, and she masculine, and that initial dialogue was understood, we would thus imitate each other, and going through that we could speak as ourselves, with an under-current of imitation. We never stopped responding to our-selves, kind of a double double play, and—we also used to drink water playing it was gin, and we got very drunk. It was fun, strange fun, but it worked, and taught me that I was more than one, and that's my storyline: dialogue of re-sponse.'

'She was blonde; pure and silky.'

Wow. I put both my hands on the table. 'Right.'

'She was,' Amelia West said, eyes in slits, 'opulent.'

'Yes,' I murmured.

'Her skin was—'

I was silent.

'—flawless and her teeth were even, and glistened white.'
'Right.'

Darkly, she said: 'She's my sister.'

'*You too*,' I whispered, and seized her wrist.

What did I mean? except the intuitive contact with—and what effect had her sister had on her? What—had—

'Fielding, you're hurting me, please, let me go.'

And as I truly said I'm sorry, and released her wrist and saw the waiter approaching us with the drinks, I had a dream of Colorado, and the foothills to the Rocky Moun-tains, and pine trees, and ghost towns, fields, and fresh-water lakes. I saw children, and animals, and birds, and flowers and a circle and an airplane in the sky. I saw my sister's face before me, and in a sudden flash my sister and I were together, painting pictures and writing poems, in Missouri, in the war of love we fought, when we were kids.

I leaned back like a blur as the waiter put our drinks before us. I glanced at Amelia and asked for menus. She nodded.

But I was there. She looked into space.

'I'm sorry,' I said, and raised my glass to her. 'Here's to you (being formal), Mrs. West, and here's to me, Mr. Dawson, and here's to the art which brought us together.'

She leaned forward a little with a face, but raised her glass; we touched rims. 'That's great,' she said softly. *Wow.*

We drank, and she asked,

'Would you please tell me about yourself?'

'Sure. Starting from where?'

'How is your new book coming.'

'The short stories?'

'Yes.' She was looking at me across the rim of her glass. Her left shoulder, in the actualization, slanted down, left elbow was on the table, hand holding the drink. Her right hand was in her lap with fingers curled.

I said, 'You've got the title story, didn't you know that? I thought I had written—'

'The book's done?'

I said, puzzled in the reverberations, and because I had submitted the information with the manuscript, 'Yes, it'll be published this September, on the West Coast.' And wanting her to return to me; lovely, complicated woman.

She paled for a moment, and then I smiled, and her face resumed its color, and for some reason I felt I was taller, lighter, with a snap-brim hat tilted in a cool wink at the future. What a bastard I am. I sipped my martini, a little disbelieving its goodness, in a way of inclusive consciousness I have, on the one hand realizing how the bartender made it, and on the other seeing level crescent eyes frame her return.

'So we're publishing the title story of a book of your stories due this September.' She blushed slightly. 'I'll drink to that, that's great. I'll mention that in the bio—that, and your first book,' she smiled.

'But actually,' she added, 'I *did* think there was another book. Are you hungry?' She laughed at the gambit for a pun.

I grinned, 'There is; yes, I am. A book of man/boy stories. Plus a long essay.'

'Is it a novel, you mean? Or—'

'No. This has no end.'

'But there is completion, no?'

I looked at her. 'Yes. It crystallizes.'

She smiled warmly. 'That's great. And an essay?'

As I nodded she asked,

'About what?'

'The tide,' I answered.

'The tide?'

'Tide, yes; you've heard of the tide?'

'Mmm, but what about it?'

'About me and it. Is that what you meant?'

'Partly. Go on.'

'Well, I aim for the future to it. I am in the future, in fact I am future.'

'I'm going to have a sandwich,' she said, 'while you fade in.'

I pointed and slowly turned my head to my right, and I said, 'I'm watching that go right over my shoulder; have something hot. I'm going to have liver and broccoli, a salad and some wine.'

She said, then, she would have roast beef, and she suddenly looked at me.

'Excuse me?'

'For what. Are you going to have wine?'

'Yes. I love wine. I thought you had said something.'

'Sorry,' and we laughed—in our storyline, and we sipped our drinks.

I said, 'It's on my mind, and I don't know why. Probably simple association, but do you know a young woman, I can't think of her name, she used to work for *Cosmopolitan*; they took a story of mine about three years ago. Susan something.'

'Sure,' Amelia said. 'We went to school together; I graduated in her freshman year.'

'Where.'

'Smith.'

'Smith? Smith in Missouri?'

'Yes, does it have sig—'

'I'm from Missouri. I'm a Missouri-smith.'

'You are? Golly!'

'Gee,' I said seriously, and she smiled: 'Boy.'

Laughed and put her hand on my arm. 'Where from?'

'Kirkwood.'

'Oh my. I've been to Kirkwood!'

'Just west of St. Louis; my main street is a bypass to—'

'Sixty-six—what street did you live on?'

'Taylor Avenue.'

'Taylor? Taylor? Where—'

'Manchester Road—'

'Yes, I remember Manchester Road—'

'You're heading west on Manchester, and about two hundred yards east of Lindburgh, you turn left onto Taylor.'

'I knew, in fact, two boys and a girl from Kirkwood.'

I faked knowing them. 'Wait a minute—'

She gave me a smile. 'Oh come on.'

I snapped my fingers, and then looked surprised. 'Come on?'

She said, 'Um hum, come on,' and I said, 'Come off it.'

She shrugged, and I said, faking I was hurt, and as if directed, 'Yeah, but you see for a minute there I was I mean I'd a swore—and then, it was like I was back home.'

'What a dreamer,' she laughed. 'Like, like when did you come to New York?'

'I knew it.'

The waiter caught my signal, and came over and we ordered; she smiled, 'I see. You thought—'

'I apprehended.'

'Well, don't be apprehensive. I know you're older than I am, you couldn't of known the kids I knew from Kirkwood.'

'True. But it always gives me a little jolt. I'm a faker, you see.'

'Me too, in a way,' she frowned. 'Particularly overseas; you meet somebody from New York—I'm from New York —and it's just *sickening* when your neighborhood is pinpointed, and you stand there on Les Champs simply *rigid*—'

I was laughing, and sipping my drink, kind of blowing bubbles, actually, mumbling, 'God, it *is* awful, Nick Schmuck, remember? and his three creep brothers on East 89th Street and the good old days?'

She laughed, 'And what are you doing tonight *being as we're from the same old neighborhood*,' she snarled, '*baby*,' and I said, 'Trying to get the hell away from the neighborhood—' and I held up my hand like Merce Cunningham.

'We have to fake and lie, because white or black, male or female, like it or not, there's a loser, a loner, a con man or a rapper on every corner, anywhere in the world.'

We nodded in agreement, and finished our drinks.

L et's have another!'
'Great!'
I got him, and we did.
With raised glasses:
'Here's to the good old neighborhood!'
'The good old neighborhood!'
'Boy, could I tell some stories.'
'Me too. Let's don't.'
It didn't matter who was saying what. We drank our drinks straight down, and I licked my lips.

We ate calmly, but hungrily, and drank wine. She was telling me that she and Susan had worked on *The Saturday Evening Post* as readers one summer vacation, and that Sue had been ambitious. I asked what had happened as Amelia asked,

'How did you meet her?'

I looked at her. 'When *Cosmopolitan* took a story, she took me to lunch.'

'Like this, you mean?'

'No.' Our eyes met. I had told Susan I wanted to make it with her.

She lowered her eyes, and gazed into her wine glass. 'May I have some more wine?'

I poured as Amelia said, 'We were very close then.'

'Then.'

'Yes,' and she looked at me over the tilting glass. 'I quit, and she stayed with them every summer, and after she graduated, she stayed with them until they folded. Remember her face?'

I murmured oh *no*. 'I liked her *very* much.'

'Exactly,' Amelia said. 'She went to some quack and he took her face off. The top layer, and she wore some kind of paste he gave her, the pain was excruciating, every night she washed her face with very hot water, and in the morning with her face like a crust she applied the paste. It was like a mask. But the acne was so deep . . .'

'Yes,' I said. 'I remember. No wonder she was so ambitious. Why didn't someone tell her about Adelle Davis?'

Amelia said, into space. 'What a writer she is.'

'So why the hell did she do it?'

'It goes way back.'

'Like acne,' I said, to illustrate the cruelty in literary gossip.

She nodded, and we sipped wine and fiddled with silverware. 'Anyway,' she said, 'it's worse than ever and she's very unhappy.'

'I liked her; very much. Sweet person.'

'Me too. Is that why you said you were sentimental?'

'Very good,' I grinned. 'Yes, literary lunches are fun.'

'It's the only part of my job I like.'

I was, in the shape of a twisted tree, suddenly irrational, and jealous of other guys—writers—being out with her, and —I kept it right there, though, though underground, and when she asked why I had said partly, I said what I felt:

'Being here with you, and because of my story and the book, it's a good book, and I have a sense about this neighborhood, and memories. Around the corner from here there used to be a bar, and whenever I went to the Modern Museum, I'd walk up this way and go to that bar; a dull, and rather woody place with pictures of old New York on the walls. It was strange because it was almost always empty, so I felt it was mine. I always had a kind of sentimental feeling—mine to remember, etc.—and around about then I wrote my first novel, which I like, and which nobody will publish, called *Open Road*, although I'm in touch with a small publisher on the West Coast, and there is a section that takes place between a young and struggling artist and a girl he meets; fiction, based on fact. He takes her to that bar, and there the relationship begins to crumble, they get into a fight and leave the bar, go to Central Park, and argue further, and separate. This neighborhood brings memories of the mid and late fifties, and my own first book to me, and being here again because of writing, enhances it; well, you can, if it ever gets published, read it.'

'And will love it. Where did you get the title?'

'Out of my sentimental head. Where else?'

'Really? Do you mean that?'

Ah teasing wicked lovely woman. 'What do you mean do I mean it? Of course I mean it.'

'Yes, but because you're sentimental that's how you got it, O.K., and what I want to know is, where from?'

'Tell me why you don't get a job someplace else.'

'But I asked first.'

'Quite so, and I second.'

The happy white knight in the dark blue suit: grinned.

The queen smiled, glanced at me, shook her head briefly, sipped wine and finished her peas. 'I don't for practical reasons. Even though it pays poorly, my job and my days are my own. I have an eight-year-old son, Philip. My husband and I are divorced, and I can leave work early to be home when Philip gets back from school. I take Thursdays off.'

'Payday? My marriage is finished, too,' I said. 'Have you had the job long?'

'Not quite a year. Why did you break up?'

'Because I didn't see her as she was. Why did you?'

She looked at me, and smiled. 'Where did you get the title *Open Road*? No, no dessert for me. I'd like some coffee.'

'None for me either. I'd like espresso—and a shot of brandy.'

'Mm! Brandy! Me too, and before you tell me, there is little I can say about your first book except that I loved it. It's very honest; yet that's clear, as your love for all those great guys—Kline, de Kooning, Pollock, Guston—and it also has mystery. Really great.'

Influenced by her spirit, I said,

'When I was a boy kids used to read a kind of moral-correct boyscout type magazine called *The Open Road for*

34

Boys, and though I never read it, the name remained with me, and as I have been addicted to vast open spaces, highways, and roads—I have walked and stood on roads and loved and lain in fields since I was a very small boy, so when I wrote the novel I called it *The Open Road* because it was completely open, in fact openly opposite from the boyscout quality of the magazine, and its forward motion, like going down a road, everyone in the book betrays each other, as if the spirit of The Open Road of America is an open road for betrayal—betrayal carte blanche—a kind of innocent golly gee green dollar stab-in-the-back hotdog doublecross and I showed the center passage to Bob Cree-ley, who liked it—this was fifteen years ago—and he said drop the article, which I did, because in the USA there is no *the* open road. It's all open, and if it ever gets published I'll send you a copy. How's that?'

'Well,' she said, 'we appear to follow a circle, of sorts; but I'd love to see it. Why don't you submit it to Grove Press?'

'Because they rejected it.'

She laughed, and I put on a sourgrapes smile.

We stood at the foot of the skyscraper and shook hands. She lifted her face like a noon moon and her level crescent eyes shone up to me. A smile flickered, and for a moment I wondered. I thanked her for lunch. And.

I almost kissed her—no, the storyline voice said, and in response I laughed, and buttoned my coat in the sudden chill spring wind. Her minidress rose—what nice legs!

Holding her dress down, she said, 'I'll call you about the drawing.'

'Look forward to it.'

I stared—suddenly she was twenty yards away floating through the glass doors. I stood in shock . . . in the winds of March . . . her perfume around me.

Then to get a fresh look, I took two steps backwards, The

Wurlitzer Rule, and looked ahead toward the subway entrance, hearing her laughter, thinking of her legs, and a shadowlike wish that came true a little too late? like me, who loves the night in the day, and feels deep nostalgia?

Probably not.

In future's storyline: I was heading toward the skyscrapers on the north side of Union Square (17th Street), when I angled in between parked cars; it was after work, and my mind was worn and I looked forward to buying the paper and getting a drink, and as I walked between the cars a motion caught me—

Glancing down, I saw a young man lying on the front seat of the closed car, licking the picture, his hand fumbling with the zipper of his pants.

His whole body was rigid, and trembling, as he licked the picture.

But his face was torn in pain, and lust, and it was like the sudden wish come true, flying up out of his unconscious and crystallized in action, that he would leap to lick the long, dangling penis of the naked boy in the full-page porno newspaper photo, and his tabloid homosexuality, it was in power and taste and touch of penis he licked to.

Regardless guilt, leaping lust in life, hidden from all except me, the secret sharer, as I went my way, bought my paper, and met my friends and Amelia in the cheerful after-work throng at the bar.

Thursday. I was standing at my desk looking at invoices and bills of lading. Go on, call her.

I did, and when she answered I said hi, thank you for a wonderful afternoon, can we meet for a drink after work?

'I'd love to,' she said, and I saw her face when she warmly said, 'But. Remember I said I had Thursdays off?'

Oh, yes. 'I forgot—sorry.'

'But I came in anyway, to catch up on some things, and am leaving in a few minutes. So—I can't,' and her voice softened: 'but thank you for calling, Fielding. I loved it.'

'Well Friday is always messy because it's Friday and everybody—'

'Look, can you come up for supper?'

'—Why,' I began, high. God, 'I'd love to.'

'Great,' she said, and gave me her Riverside Drive address. 'You can meet Philip. Do you like baseball?'

'Are you aware with whom you are speaking?' I heard her laughter.

'Philip loves baseball. I got him a glove for Christmas.'

'Well,' I said. 'Yes. I'm pretty crazy about baseball, mostly about—' (you) '—that Met shortstop Bud Harrelson,' I laughed. 'You know me, Al,' I snickered, to me.

'Ring Lardner,' she smiled. 'About seven-thirty?'

'Seven-thirty. Can I bring some hooch?'

'No, if we—'

'I'll go out and get some. Shall I bring my bat? I have a Louisville Slugger. 33-inch DiMaggio. How old did you say he was?'

'DiMaggio? Can't say. Philip's eight.'

I thought; either. Remember eight? 'Boy,' I said. 'Eight indeed, and seven-thirty it is.'

I hung up slowly, and stared out the window, and whispered Jesus, looking at John at the typewriter directing language to Mr. Ashcraft in Los Angeles. 'We're putting a tracer on your order,' John's fingers flew, but he was looking at me. I had a big smile on, and he asked,

'What's up.'

I told him.

'You sure work fast,' he smiled, and went back to his type-writer sounding like seventeen crickets chasing Mr. Ash-craft across the wastelands of L.A., also responding, per-haps, a little angrily at me being happy in that blasted office, couldn't blame him; I was pretty much up in the air.

The Hudson River lay beyond the lighted cliffs, and as I walked along the curving avenue I felt a mingling of the past with the future, as her future face and speaking voice blended with the neighborhood faces and voices of my past. I pulled my scarf tighter, and the late March winds from the river sent scraps of paper along street and sidewalks like independent spirits of voices of friends—the anxious laughter of my ex-wife and I with the drunken bookstore owner who thought I was a great writer in the days when the only people who read my stories were the characters at the bar; so the winds of March. I felt nostalgia, and apprehension, and ahead then, I saw a shaft of blue-white light on the sidewalk, cast from a building on the corner, and as I walked toward it I had the sudden reverse sensation that I could be in any city in the world, feeling what a million men before me felt, and would feel, while in continuity in an unseen apartment a woman was preparing supper for the two of us—for me, for herself. For us.

The clock in the flower shop said ten to eight. I asked the florist where the address on Riverside Drive would be, and as I bought the roses he explained it. I thanked and paid him, accepted the funnel of flowers and walked out of the blue-white light into darkness, crossed the street going uphill under an awning, turned left at the corner and descended a concrete hill toward the park and river beyond. The number, when I got there, was above the door, engraved in a faceless cement oval, and the pleasant-faced doorman said yessir.

'Mrs. West,' I said, without expression, so as not to get in a talk with him. '12 L. She's expecting me.'

I told him my name and he stepped back, and pushed a button on the number bank, and in static mentioned my name, and nodded to me as she responded, and he took a step toward the inner door which was open, and as he clicked off, he gestured,

'O.K., Mr. Dawson, the elevator's down the corridor on your left and around the corner to your right.'

I thanked him, and walked in a yellowish light made by small wall bulbs; cool yellow-stained marble floors, pillars, walls, with gilded mirrors punctuated by long, bulky marble-topped tables on curved legs with claw feet, 1913 solidarity forever was intact and it angered and depressed me. I turned the corner of the cave: glossy dark-brown doors with heavy brass knobs flanked the wall on my left and on my right I saw the elevator door with a brass knob and a diamond-shaped glass set in at eye level, chicken-wire inset between the plates of glass, and I pushed the button and the door wiggled open, I got on, pushed 12, the door wiggled shut, the machine wiggled, shuddered, and jiggled, shivered, shook, and with a lurch began to climb up, with me inside, trapped like a rat, face bleached and feet braced, hands gripping the side rails, terrified, and when the thing reached the twelfth floor and went through its stopping tricks and the door skiddled open, and I got off, I hoped I wouldn't have to go out for anything—as I had promised —walking down the marble floor between beige and blue walls toward her glossy brown door with 12 L in gold above the small round peephole, I felt a little hysterical, and in the apprehension of wanting to see her and what would happen and being so late, when I rang the bell, a high-speed dentist's drill sound, I was very tense, angry and al-

44

most frightened—then I saw her in my mind, it released it, and I felt the laughter I like so much: this could only happen to me, and I experienced a humility and warmth that compared to a touch of self *thankyou* and felt, therefore, I was my own Saint of Touch Me, and when she opened the door and saw my expression, with flowers, a warmth came off her face like a circle, which I entered as she said come in, and there was a soft soft darkness.

And I later rationalized: I think she did it to let me know herself—to remind me, rather—and to also slightly keep me alert, because in my entrance it was obvious I trusted the place of darkness while I apologized for being so late and asked where Philip was and she said in bed, and before I could get my cigarettes out of my raincoat pocket, she had, she was taking the roses out of the paper and walking away from the door—which had just closed—my raincoat and scarf were in the coat closet to the immediate left in the wall, how the fuck she did it, I'll never—she made a self laugh softly, and as she put roses into a beautiful pewter vase, she thanked me, in the warmest tone of the girl in the experience of the woman loving roses,

'Let's,' in a kind of echo, 'have a drink!'

'Wonderful. May I look around?'

'Sure. What would you like?'

I told her, and *again* understood darkness: an archway entered another room, and beyond that the bright lights of her living room, yet the foyer, where I was standing as if facing the future, was then a corridor of the past: walls lined with photographs and drawings; some large, some small. There were gallery announcements, and a very large photo reproduction of an egg in an eggcup over a folded gateleg table. Avedon? But some of the artwork was square, some were oval, and some rectangular; some were the hard-edged black and white or brilliantly colored slick fashion type, and some were old sepia tone, and some were so immediately away from my experience I couldn't recognize them, and had to bend close. In gray and slightly blurred photo tones a group of men sat at a table smoking cigars. In straw hats, relaxed and smiling. I heard her in the kitchen, and went to the closet and got my cigarettes from my raincoat, and closed the door and looked around the room, again puzzled.

I saw lots of pictures of children, and as I gazed at them, wondering which one was Philip, and in the others who was father, and mother, and which was her ex-husband and where was sister? I realized she was standing beside me, ice tinkling in its glass, and as I turned to her and took the drink, and walked into the living room, I said,

'Really interesting, these pictures. Where's the one of you?'

Suddenly in her silence.

I saw my roses, in the pewter vase on a long low elegant marble-topped table, on a parquet floor about six inches away from the edge of a brightly complicated crimson, ultramarine, and black Oriental rug, and in front of a big beautiful richly covered cream-colored sofa, I saw a display of food almost like flowers, in dishes and with silverware and napkins and little things that so impressed me I gaped and felt Huck Finn.

Cheeses and sauces, and crisp vegetables—there were stalks of celery a foot and a half long, and a small enameled dish held celery hearts, which I loved; I saw artichokes, and boy did my juices flow! There were radishes, of course, ice cold to the touch, and there were olives of all kinds, and figs, and herring in sour cream, it was a picnic, it was a feast as cheeses stood in blocks, and balls, and in little triangular boxes on cutting boards; and an uncut loaf of pumpernickel bread, and an uncut loaf of Jewish rye bread; and little differently shaped crackers; and there was more, like the dish of little round red tomatoes, and the dish of peeled cucumbers sliced thin lengthwise, flanked by a small orange and green and blue-lipped pitcher reminding me of the set we had at home that the Russian ambassador had given my grandmother at the St. Louis

World's Fair. A little gem of a pitcher, and it would hold vinegar and tarragon, I knew, and I was right.

And under the eaves of the huge cut-glass bowl bursting with the celery stalks, I saw in a little shallow dish: black caviar—God, Jesus—

Amelia was, literally, radiant, and in my hillbilly astonishment, she seemed, as we sat on and then sank into the sofa as I scooped caviar onto a little wheat wafer, and handed it to her, and she said no, I had some, this is for you, it was, she was inexplicable, Shiva, she was in such calmness, and I said, guiltily,

'You mean when I didn't show up, you had some.'

'Not at all; I nibbled while fixing it.'

I ate the caviar and the wafer, it was delicious, and I sipped my drink, and offered her a cigarette which she took, and as I lit it I said, almost hysterically,

'Come on, I can't—stand eating alone;' she made a cool smile.

'In a bit. Thanks.'

'For what?'

'Asking; and for the cigarette. And the light.'

I mumbled, working over an artichoke: 'You're welcome. Terrific.'

'I'm glad,' she murmured, putting out the cigarette, and slowly, so I could see what she was doing, she prepared a radish with salt, and ate it with a smooth glowing hunger, and *class*, Amelia had class, the effortlessness of a forest river, she was the moving nature rippling across the surface of her power from all the way down below, and a gray and black striped cat came into the room and eyed the food, and me. I looked at it.

'Tell me of March tide,' Amelia said.

I sat back dabbing my lips with a paisley paper napkin, sipped my drink and lit a cigarette; in the line of the story, I wondered how, the cat jumped on the Camembert and I said, while lifting the cat out,

'Not yet. Have to do more.'

'More—'

'Work. I'm not where I'm going. I'm still being led.' The cat appeared on her lap.

'It's too new, you mean?'

'Well, or I'm too new. Something. I'm not where I'm it seems obviously going, yet. I'll know, though.'

'Are you self-conscious again? Don't be. And when you get there?' She stroked the cat. The cat was asleep. Was the cat asleep, or dozing? Yes, the cat was asleep! Get on!

'Yes. I know something is in my future, and I go for it.' Mumble.

'It doesn't take much to make you self-conscious. I'm lost.'

I looked at the sleeping cat and answered her questions feeling her coming into me because we were getting intuitive again, yet I wasn't exactly sure I wanted that, or was I? and I wondered about her confusion. But that too was how I was.

I explained: 'I don't mean to apprehend and confuse you; I'm sorry. It's how I write, and crystallize. I don't end.'

She said, 'I'll read the first book again, and watch it more closely,' as a cream-colored cat came into the room and looked at me, and as it came toward the food, we—me and it—watched each other.

'I have the feeling you're going to ask me what I ask myself,' the cat disappeared under the table, 'so to me your voice is mine, and to answer it I answer myself with a kind of solid knowledge that I *know* could be you,' and the cat appeared in my lap, 'as well as my voice could be within you, responding to your questions,' and the cat jumped onto the cheddar, I threw the cat on the floor, 'I mean you've heard people say, "I was just going to say that," or "I was thinking the same thing," etc.,' and the cat gave me a scathing look, and folded up asleep on the rug. The other cat woke up and looked at the sleeping cat, and Amelia said it sounded like I was being defensive, and maybe I didn't want to talk about March tide, but also maybe she still didn't understand, and I said, Well, God-damnit—

'I'm stupid,' she added, and I was angry at that and frowned hard at her, and she amended: 'My failing. Can you make it clearer?'

The cat in her lap made a leap for the cheese, 'FOR CHRIST'S SAKE!' I yelled, knocked it sprawling onto the floor, 'We want a dialogue, so we build a dialogue within us, and' the cat walked toward the doorway, glanced at me over its shoulder, made a little hiss, and fell asleep on the parquet floor, 'after a sort of habit formation of asking and answering, an inner ear gets to know the tones and rhythms of the dialogue, so when I heard you asking me, it was as if I was asking myself, and when I ask myself the questions you just have, *I* get no answers, so the piece on March tide is still too new, yes, and I'm not far along enough yet to know exactly what I mean or what I'm doing, and this is how I write. I listen to it.'

I could see her thinking then why didn't you say that in the first place, and she said, instead, 'I'm lost. You're too intense.'

'No, I'm too convoluted,' and I finished my drink, put it on the table, and saw her move, slowly to keep in vision, like a Blake poem, pick it up as I said, 'I know a reporter for *The Tides*, and once I said something and I mean something normal, personal I guess, but nothing cosmic, and all the blood ran out of his face. Why.'

She looked at me with the glass in her hand. 'What did you say to him?'

'I don't remember exactly, we were a little drunk;' both cats quickly left the room; 'it was something about Ron Hunt, the then second baseman for the Mets. My book had just come out and the reporter was thinking about an article we could do on the New York art world, together, they're waiting for you to go to the kitchen, no? They must be hungry. I didn't know cats liked cheese.'

'They'll eat anything.'

'I see, and well, the baseball season was over and everyone knew the Mets were going to trade Hunt to the Dodgers, and we talked about that, he liked Hunt, and I said I did too and he said Hunt really had something, and I said Hunt reminded me of my past, so that I was sentimental about Hunt, because they were tougher in those days, and I had witnessed them, and he nodded, and I said when I'd write my book about my childhood and baseball and love it would be like Ron Hunt—and hopefully his, too.'

'The tough past and the players?'

'Yes. To be, or not. But it must be.'

'Nothing cosmic of course, just a little mysticism. And baseball?' she smiled, and the thread of her smile floated around my eyes,

And baseball.

That's love, too; I was suddenly expanding and listening in a vertical crystal field seeing her smile, in a crazy lust for space and open roads and the warm feminine aura—and baseball, and in a nascent knowing I returned upward in the presence of another: I stared at her, and when our eyes met, I saw sparks.

Whispering: *Philip.*

She rose like smoke in her soft and double laughter, and left me sitting there like a pale white cat—pretty Krazy, easily outwitted, gazing wide-eyed into space with a comic smile, well what baseball was to me Philip is to her future as she disappeared from the room t-t-that's a-all f-f-folks her tinkling voice in a yet edgy laugh reaching me,

'Where have you been?'

'That's my line,' I said, and put out the cigarette, and as I ate a black olive I thought I would open my mind to Philip because whatever I said when I spoke about baseball sent her to Philip, and there I was thinking about baseball. I thought that was pretty nifty the way she got that in; proof she likes you, a voice said; strangely, I smelled the roses, and the air seemed to clear of the me me me.

I saw a painting, on the wall above the false white fireplace, and below it, on the mantel beneath the painting, I saw a black and brown striped cat sprawled, and asleep. I saw floor-to-ceiling bookcases on both sides of the fireplace, and in a sense the room became more clear, but it was as if the painting were part of the cat, or the cat part of the painting, or of the act: a cat, the act, and the painting, and I had a remarkable feeling that I was in one of my own stories.

Painted deliberately blurred, a dusky pink ball sat next to a mustard-colored pyramid on a square but slanting ocher table and underneath the table a large gray rat shape lurked: each image softly darkly outlined. The distance beyond was an ocher and pink desert.

The cat's tail twitched. A point of light, like an amoeba, tumbled into a flash and I looked at the cat, the painting, and turned my head and saw her eyes in the brilliant light pouring up through the lampshade at the end of the sofa as she came through a different door. Silver and gray and black October eyes in happiness, and I grinned as she passed quite a small painting of a pink bat smiling, wings in, perched on top of a mustard-colored pyramid on a Surrealistic desert. She drifted flowing into the deep sofa and handed me the drink as a cat appeared in her lap.

I laughed.

But there was something else. On my right—beckoning. I looked.

Two windows overlooked downtown Manhattan. Window shades and window curtains moved softly, gently above a Victorian loveseat, and to our right at the end of the sofa, a large Victorian rolltop desk, top up, revealing a portable Olivetti, waiting. A highbacked armchair faced the desk. The ghost and Mrs. Muir. Two wing chairs flanked a small marble-topped table in front of the fireplace before us. The cream-colored cat lay under the wing chair on the left, tail curled around a chair leg, and then I caught the winding relativity of it, and where it went: invisible threads ran from the cat under the chair to the black and brown cat on the mantel and to the black and gray cat in her lap, like the lines to and from Amelia and myself and to Philip, in his little bed in the room through the wall behind us, sleeping in his own thread to her.

But it was the open window, that remained.

I sipped my drink and made a little smile; it was beginning, just coming into form, and when I asked,

'Where are the pictures of you?'

She surprised me. 'There aren't any.'

'But why?'

'I don't like pictures of me.'

I was about to say I would, when I stopped, and she said,

'I know you do,' slightly blushed and finished her drink. 'I'd like another. Are you hungry?'

'Yes,' I answered. 'But we have the best part of the evening ahead of us, and I'm having some remarkable exper—'

She laughed outright. 'Yes! It *is* a funny place.' And looked at the cat on the mantel. 'You.'

Had the cat signed the lease? Not a whisker moved.

'They sleep,' she said to outer space. 'They eat, and sleep, shit and play wall to wall.'

'Wall to wall? Isn't that a novel by Douglas Woolf?'

Again she laughed. 'Funny! I hadn't made the association—you're right!' She pointed to the walls and the bookcases, and sure enough, I saw cat tracks. I rose and followed them from wall to wall. Some of the books were torn, and feeling strange tremors from Algernon Blackwood, I sat down as she said I should regard it as amusing. Funny. Cats are funny.

'They sure are. They'll wreck the joint.'

'Noooo,' she murmured. 'They love to play—that's all!'

'You ought to put up hurdles, and start races, who gets in first wins an extra spoon of mackerel.'

We laughed, and I said, 'What I think is funny is how they relate to the paintings.'

She looked at the paintings, and nodded, with a slight frown, yes, she said, and put her hand to her throat, fingered a peace necklace, and murmured actually this whole apartment is funny, looked into the upper lefthand corner of the room with an inner chuckle, and then glanced at me.

'I've come to like it.'

You mean you like but fear it, I thought. She finished her drink, ate a black olive, and after I ate a heap of Camembert on a small circular wheatie crisp really good, I drank the icy vodka straight down, and felt in total command. She said,

'Let's have one more and then supper, O.K.?'

'Absolutely. Can I help?'

'Yes, as a matter of fact. Lift the leaf of the table. It's a gateleg and don't let the noise it makes disturb you. Philip sleeps through anything. And if you'd like, you can light the candles.'

She rose, and turned, looking on a downward angle at me, suddenly beautiful, yet aloof and even arch, body so simply elegantly wrapped in the once-around dress, belted at the waist, beautifully yellow flowered; I saw her feet in gold slippers.

Rising from a plunging neckline her throat was fully striking, and soft and vulnerable, into the drawn strength of her neck, and her firm solid skull, and for an instant she was startled by my direct gaze, and as she left the room I had a last glance to remember: The Amelia Factor articulated in the black spark circling outwards: Watch out, Fielding, I'm Amelia. Not you. Sensitive lips fixed gravely the blur line across her strong jaw.

I leaned against the kitchen doorjamb, and she handed me the drink. A cat was asleep in the kitchen doorway. I pointed to a photograph of a woman in furs, and we stood, looking at it.

'Is this?'

'My mother.'

'She looks like a movie star, like Harlow.'

'Yes, she did; beautiful, and true.'

'Was—was she true?'

'What you said was true. Mother was anything but, except to herself, and even then . . . and yes, she was beautiful.'

The photo was softly blurred, and the woman, head thrown back in furs and long vulnerable throat fully exposed, looked straight into the lens with the hard warm yet contemptuous smile of self-worship, 1928, with the secret of sex and power keyed beneath the furs. Long fingers touched the pulse in her neck.

'Wow,' I said.

Amelia nodded, and I set up the leaf which screeched and screamed and I saw candles standing high in cut-glass holders and I lit them, and soft light flickered, to be warm for us at supper, and we went into the living room with three cats at our heels, we sat down, talked a while and sipped our drinks.

'Where'd you get the dress?'

'Altman's. Do you like it?'

The three cats stationed themselves.

'It's beautiful.'

She laughed a self laugh. 'Thanks. I shop, when I shop, all over town. There's no particular store.'

Cats stretched, curled, draped, sighed, and slept.

'You resemble her.'

Amelia looked at the floor. 'You should see my sister.' Anxiety suppressed. 'Mother's dead. She died when I was fourteen.'

Her eyes were down, her face was grim, and close to expressionless. She was just sitting. A beautiful puppet of a woman, and a girl. We didn't speak until she looked at me, feeling I guess she had to finish it, and she said, lowly,

'She committed suicide.'

I bit my lip, and held my breath as I made a fist and saw a crimson glassy sheet approach my eye, and I had a taste of blood. I said, 'I'm sorry,' and Amelia sipped her drink, cupped it in her hands and held it in her lap.

'She jumped.'

I had an echo of a scream, as in a roaring landscape as she put her hand on her throat, saying Dad died two years later.

Involuntary. In childhood fractured, and then murdered, and I said, 'If you want to tell me, I'm—I'm here.'

'There's nothing to tell. You write—you,' she murmured, 'feel too much.'

'I can't help hearing you,' I said, and knew she was saying it to me. A chancy thing for her, to speak to such an angry and fearing stranger. Her grief appeared and there she was, head lowered. My vision blurred, and I wiped my eyes, cleared my throat, and said her name.

She looked up, and our eyes met. I raised my glass to her, and said,

'To us.'

We toasted, and she managed a smile. 'Shall we eat?'

My heart melted in my up-and-away being true to her, and also to me, and we had heard each other.

'Swell,' I said, and felt a flash.

We were in tableau, in her apartment, in the clamor of nations, and swarms of people, a man and a woman together somewhere in the world had a warm and lovely supper by candlelight, with cold white wine. Her eyes sparkled and my heart was pounding—I, the man on the silver screen. Trapped again, again, like it had never happened before, and it hadn't—it had, but not like this, not like this with her.

Mushrooms and wine sauce with chicken and vegetables and us, the cold wine, the salad all so dreamy it was a little supernatural. The silverware, the plates, the wine glasses! And the candlesticks and the quality of Scrooge seeing Morley in the doorknocker, I saw faces in the intricate designs on knife and fork and spoon handles, which seemed to blend with the magic of cut-glass amber wine glasses, gold-rimmed with stems as long and as delicate as drinking straws, appeared sparkling and prismatic, and on the periphery of the refractions, her October eyes glinted, and so did my own green eyes and the after taste of the wine, as dancing, in its own voice whispered *more, more,* like the whirl of the waltz in the vision I had that dawn so many years ago, standing at the rail of the troopship in freezing cold and sleet off the coast of France, as we approached the Channel, I was the first one on deck for morning chow and in dim first dawn I saw a yacht with lights ablaze, anchored close by, and I watched it slip behind us in fog and gloom and through portholes saw men and women waltzing, and heard the faintest sweeping, mystic sound of the great Mozart in sea drift, *more,* and I filled her glass, and let its rim kiss her, I too passionate to dare and too passionate to make it obvious, so I kept my face in check—did she know? She knew, and asked, brightly,

'Editors?'

'Do you want to ruin a great meal? Why were you so anxious to know where I got my title—you mean—?' I asked suddenly.

'Yes, I used to read *The Open Road for Boys*—it was still around when I was young, and I mean,' she faked appearing hurt, 'just exactly what I said.'

Well,' I grinned. 'Let me see. Where was I?'

She pointed at me.

'It appeared to be France,' and then I apologized. 'You mean editors, well, I guess it's a defensive stance for them. I'm so full I can hardly talk.'

'How about some coffee? Brandy?'

I looked up, out of the left-hand corners of my eyes to where the line begins—from left to right—to read, and made a complicated grateful laugh. Yes, that would be wonderful. 'Can I help?'

'Not a chance,' and taking nothing but my words with her, she vanished into kitchen noises. I looked around, wondering if it all was true—and saw the photographs. Photographs: mechanical imitation of memory. Attempt at keeping a face in view, or a view in face; substitute for the inner eye which knows no forgetting the woman in furs who paved the way for Amelia. I felt a sequence of responses to my feeling for Amelia's future, my feeling of the what, not the when, and I let what I saw and felt be a field for my responses to her, so on entrance, she would connect, and yet I also felt fake, in a painted hero's wish that I could help, but how, to prepare her for my story-line? So. Old manipulator, I, sipped wine; well, I thought, let's keep the tone and skip the therapy, and while I rose and looked at the pictures letting the wish in each photograph be known to me, this was the Pinocchio Gambit: if they could only be human. She appeared with the coffee and brandy, and I felt striking brandy glasses ringing as she was asking would I like to go in the living room? It startled me, and I smiled.

'Let's stay. It's nice here.'

I can't explain it, a way she was rippling pleasure-leaves and grass blades in her fields. She smiled, and after I put a bit of brandy in each glass, I raised mine.

'To you.'

She, hers: 'To you.'

We sipped, and I emptied my glass into my coffee while she laughed—and did likewise.

We smoked my French cigarettes.

'What do you mean a defensive stance.'

I confessed, 'I've always wanted to write a book about it, or a long and *furious* essay.'

'You should. You could do it. They hate writers.'

'Boy, do they,' and in the helpless thought, I became a little depressed. 'Where to begin?'

'From the beginning.'

'*That's* what I meant before. You do say what I am and am about to say, see?' I finger-tapped a dance on the tabletop and laughed, angrily: 'They have the power, the writer doesn't. The writer is helpless. You know, that guy changed Heller's book from Catch-18 to Catch-22, because Uris's Mila 18 was out, and the change missed the subtle charming and tragic link from the text to the title, Catch-18, perfect because of its regressive undertone, the protagonist Yossarian often behaving like 18, but the editor, with a tin ear and a starry-eyed ambition youthfully WILD about alliteration like it's the craziest thing going, called it Catch-22—22, get it? In the trade, you know, Heller's book is considered to be the editor's. What'sisname?'

She shook her head. I was a little breathless.

'Well they call it his book, not Heller's.' I sat back in a grim dreamy silence, remembering what editors had done to me. And publishers. She looked at me, and lowering her head and raising the coffee cup to her lips, her eyes had a quality of eclipse.

I said, 'To hell with it.'

'No! Go on—'

'No, I get so—'

'But so do I! Please, tell me what *you* think, it helps me!' Her eyes hardened. 'What happened at Grove.'

'Don Allen liked it, Rossett rejected it.'

'But isn't that—'

'Yes, routine. *Esquire* lost seven stories of mine and they couldn't figure out why I was so pissed. Seven stories at one shot. They're so involved, they're so uncaring, vacuous, blank. There's a way to reject a manuscript, why insult the writer? The writer is helpless, as Rudy Wurlitzer says, writers are treated like women. Editors wine you, court you and dine you and after you're fucked it's all over, they're not interested. The writer can't get them—unless, of course,' I said softly, 'face to face. Revenge is sweet,' I said, and suddenly I leered, a touch of glee in candlelight. I said,

'I know what a *little* revenge is.'

Eyes blazing, 'I'm dying!' she cried. 'For Christ's sake, tell me!'

I told her the story about one editor who wanted to shake my hand in a bar, and No, I said, I wouldn't touch him, and there he was with his hand out. Krim was there, and much impressed. A small act that felt great.

'It's their editorial ego that won't permit—because they're so jealous and insecure—they'll not permit any manuscript to pass through their hands unchanged, they'll change a comma to a semicolon, or a colon to a comma like a thoughtless child challenging the true authority of the writer, and the writer who lets them do what they will is as guilty as the editor. But the editor can't leave it alone. Otherwise he's only a part of the medium of publishing, and that's anathema. They all know each other, too. It's a club. And most books read the same, have the same feel, because they're structured by an editorial process that resembles clubhouse logic, dictated by publishers and/or corporations who follow an invisible vindictive code they never have to defend because they're never challenged, and the last person in the world they'd consider thinking about is that fall-guy sucker the writer, who signed that contract. They're horrible people, all of them, and they're bland—they're nothing but a pack of white dogs up in skyscrapers barking at high noon for a justified buck and the manipulative power of editorial prestige.'

'GREAT! BRAVO! *Terrific.*' She clapped her hands, face brilliant; so vivid.

I said:

'So fuck 'em.' And I raised my coffee.

She too: '*Fuck* 'em,' and we touched rims, and in soft unison, droned, fuuuck 'em.

And we drank.

'Well, with *one* exception,' and we touched hands in laughter.

Laughing still, she sliced an apple, offering me a hunk, which I took, and seeing a pear in the bowl, sliced it, and offered it, yes, and we swapped slices and hummed in our throats and ate and in thoughtful, humorous silence, both of us a little drunk, we had a little more coffee, and a little more brandy. I asked,

'Where is the john?'

I followed her instructions, and went, and pissed in the toilet alongside the sink by the bathtub/shower loaded with toy boats, ducks, blocks, balls and rings and a long-handled scrub brush, washcloths, and towels, all awry, normal, actual, therefore touching. I flushed the toilet, washed my hands and looked into the mirror. I was drunk, in there, and I smiled as I dried my hands, and going into the hallway tripped over a sleeping cat, I pitched forward, but caught myself on a closet doorknob across the hall from me while the cat made an outcry and zipped out of sight.

She was standing by the table. 'Let's sit in the living room.'

'Swell, I almost broke my neck, never mind. Cats.' I got my coffee cup and joined her in the living room on the sofa by the cluttered, magnificent display of food on the low table as she put the brandy down, and—in her way—vanished into the kitchen for the coffee pot.

The coffee was hot, and we laced it with brandy and she asked about March tide. I smiled warmly. I said, kindly, letting the room rise,

'Isn't a little a lot?'

'Mmm.'

It seemed we smoked too many or just enough cigarettes, because the room was warm and smoky and sweet in coffee/brandy fume, soft, deep sofa, and all cats sleeping.

'The cats,' I said.

And the paintings, the photographs, the open window overlooking downtown Manhattan, which began to haunt me though I didn't know it, and the walls, and the sleeping boy in the next room, receded a few inches and the air of night and city hovered around us, as we talked about where we'd been born, gone to school, of childhood, briefly. Briefly, heart pounding, I said her name, the window disappeared forever, our eyes met and held and I flowed and kissed her as she accepted and embraced me, and all sparkling veins became an artery of our one power. Let's do it. O.K.—

thrashing grass

as her body left my hands, I followed her through a door which opened before us, and as I entered, closed, and I whispered,

'The candles.'

Lighted by my return, the room glowed warm, and as

I turned I saw a naked breast in shoulder tilt and in one motion I saw her dress slide off as her hand slid her little bikini panties off, I undressed and we were naked and only partly conscious, as we fell she guided my erect cock into her upward-moving, beckoning vaginal fire and I went all the way up into the expanding uteral cave as her cervix pressured and I arrived at cave's end and the one hot Braille blood dot to touch and nestle in my cock's eye, up in, I caressed her everywhere, and she caressed me slowly with her clitoris, and secretions flowed, as tips of our tongues touched, her left leg slid under my right one, and in a gathering circular darkness her thighs gripped my balls against her, writhing steaming and I licked her neck and ear and caught a sudden fantastic scent of perfume, what is that, ah God, as I slowly pulled out and slowly went in and she made a low, long gasp, that perfume, it is so *female*,

'*Femme*,' she laughed, and I too, and we both laughed, so intensely together we almost became each other, her hands stroked my hair and my head and my body, tenderly, as powerfully as her clitoris, and I ran my fingers down her back and held her ass, and we went out and in kissing hotly, darkly into the dream-flow.

I softly cried out, it all came and it was our voices, I had a sense of nightwind, and stony fields, dimly the pneuma took form and I heard her nature cry in a distant whisper calling for, and finding, itself, and we sighed, and as if in a spiritual tilt we tumbled, and floated, and in a long slant of touch and soft tide, we, as I kissed her shoulder and she murmured wordless words, slowly, dreamily, embraced, we slipped off into sleep, sleep God with it.

On a wave, I opened my eyes a crack: some thing moved. I blinked into focus, her nakedness—I saw, she had a lean lithe body, wide at the hips sliding into bed next to me with a bottle of wine and the corkscrew, the covers were over us, and as she handed me the corkscrew, I murmured,

'I'll get used to that.'

'I love it. The other bottle was empty. Would you?'

I opened the wine, Amelia; and filled the long-stemmed gold-rimmed amber glasses, and we lay on our stomachs and drank beside each other against the small pillows I liked, in her splendid large bed. I looked at her, and she was flushed, happy and youthful-looking, and in the candlelight she looked about twelve years old. There wasn't a line on her face, and I smiled, happily romantic,

'By candlelight, you know, you look like you're twelve.'

She stretched her whole body, and curled up against me, and as she put an arm around me, and moved her body powerfully against me, and with a smile straight from Egypt, she softly laughed, and, very clever woman, murmured in my ear,

'Then we will live by candlelight.'

The wine glass was to my lips, but when I saw the little flicker I put it down with my left hand as my right hand drew her close, and we kindled and caught—fire and dream—and again made love. God.

After, in peace I gently lifted her face to mine, and in a long tide, kissed her. We lay together without moving, after.

'You'll come for supper tomorrow?'

I said sure and felt her lips as she kissed my chest, and as she ran her hand from my shoulder to my knee, she rose, saying,

'I want some wine.'

I rose, too, and we sat cross-legged on the bed, with the ashtray between us, and drank wine. The bottle was almost empty, and then it was.

She said, 'You can't stay, I'm sorry. He comes in every night.'

'I know. It's all right.'

'I'm *glad* you came,' she whispered. Her eyes and lips glowed toward me.

'Did you wonder?'

'Yes. Did you?'

'Yes, in the flower shop, and afterwards on the way. The territory, I mean this part of town, has many memories for me.'

'With your wife?'

'Yes.'

'What happened.'

'I was fucked up—lost within myself, but wait—do you mean that?'

'What do—' and she laughed. 'You're a tease. *Touché*'

We laughed together, and I said, 'Come, let's be close before I go.'

We finished the wine and put the glasses and the ashtray on the night tables, and lay beside each other, her head on my shoulder, in silence and candlelight, for a warm brief tide, flowing, in a lazy turn above the lake.

I stood by the hangar and looked across the highway into the sky above the lake. It was really a beautiful warm day, hot in fact, but the flatness of Illinois seemed to drive it right back up into its sky-self, just as I looked down on it I could feel it rising. Then I saw the Cub. Its pilot was with my sister. Unique.

I stood, hoping she would come down, although I felt her up there with him, not down here with me, I wanted it normal, so I could go up, and she to know what I felt too, when I came down.

Intuition: in the touch of the doorbell something on the other side, seventeen after seven and the second hand swept around the circle. I smiled, raised my finger to buzz, hesitated an instant and then jabbed it once lightly, and on the sharp nerve-drill sound the door was flung open and the boy stood breathing hard, looking up at me eyes blazing, hands out at his sides, fingers curved, eight years old and stocky, barefoot in a faded blue bathrobe: handsome face frantic with expectancy, and when I smiled to him he made a sound like a tree splitting, and seeing the flowers in my hand, his face darkened.

'Mommy,' he said, between his teeth, 'he's here.'

'Hi!' I heard her voice drift slowly. 'Come in!'

She appeared behind him, radiant, hands out to take daisies and my coat and scarf, and as I stepped into the apartment my raincoat and scarf vanished along her hands into the closet, the flowers flew somewhere, and as she and I clasped hands a little shyly, she said,

'Philip, say hi to Fielding.'

He nearly thumped his chest. 'YEAH!' he yelled. 'PHILIP!'

'Wow,' I laughed. 'How are you doing?'

He lightly snarled something, and then laughed darkly. 'Good.'

68

Again I, as in entrance the night before, felt a darkness and as she *had* taken my daisies, coat and scarf asking me if I wanted a drink, I realized to enter her apartment and journey into her living room was as to pass through a photographed past phase, and that the living room was the room of our future living. Ours?

Yes, and you will work on your books downtown.

As she asked me, while I nodded, if I wanted a drink, I nodded yes, Philip, not knowing—in conflict—who was I if I was I, and why, and if so: who was I to be here, for him? He followed his mother into the kitchen and I went into the living room and again witnessed the fantastic antipasto. On the low marble-topped table in front of the large, soft sofa, where I sat, and had a wheat wafer with a large gob of stinky Limburger cheese, delicious, and feeling a pair of eyes I turned, and saw Philip's face around the doorjamb, eyes blazing in the downward shaft of light beneath the lampshade, eyes given a luminous glassy quality, and as our eyes met, he slipped out of view and Amelia came flowing in with the drinks, gave me mine, and sat down. She leaned forward to put out her cigarette. I put my hand up her dress between her legs and kissed her.

On contact her lips trembled, and I sat back erect, smiling with her, and turning in my position so I could face her. We toasted each other, and sipped, I offered her a cigarette which she accepted and I lit both as all three cats came into the room, took positions, and Philip came in behind them and stood in front of the low table, behind celery stalks, facing me. He looked at me squarely and ate a green olive, made a face and spit the olive bits and pit on the floor. Amelia sipped her drink and said a little something to him, and as he twisted whimpering, he turned and kicked one of the cats. Amelia picked up the olive remains and put them in an ashtray, and as the cats fled, she sat back on the sofa, sat altogether back, and I looked at her in such a way she smiled coolly, and lowered her eyes, and Philip, frowning, made a grumpy apology and stood beside

Amelia's crossed knees, on the other side of her from me, and he watched me look into his mother's eyes.

He gave her knee a shove, and as she moved her thighs away from the arm of the sofa, Philip climbed up and sat between her and the arm and looked at me gravely, while she and I toasted the three of us, the drink was very good, had she learned from men? and Philip shoved her hip and she looked at him, and as he said,

'Mommy! I want to ask you something,'

he was looking at me.

A look square at the alien.

'All right,' she said.

'Move over,' he murmured.

'The stage is set,' I smiled.

As I looked at Amelia, the plot, she smiled warmly, thickens, and laughed after I mentioned Sherlock.

She moved over, and he leaned back silently and looked at the ceiling as we talked and then his eyes swung again to me and he sat forward and put his hands on her legs, I envied that, and he looked at me. I had an artichoke, and as a cat jumped up next to the cheese board I swung at it, it ducked and I missed, Philip laughed, the cat looked at me in alarm, I picked it up and tossed it on the floor muttering for Christ's sake, cats eating cheese, and Philip said, his face a little like a glowing lantern, skin flushed, eyes like candles,

'Maybe he likes cheese,' he said.

My move. 'Do you?' I asked.

He studied me a little, and Amelia watched us. Philip said, carefully,

'With crackers. Do you?'

'Sure,' I said. 'Want a piece?'

He was weighing his decision, and his face hardened as he headed toward the piece of cheese on a cracker I held out, and he stopped, thinking we were wishing he wasn't there, and I said, evenly,

'Your mother tells me you like baseball.'

He rejected the gambit, didn't take the cheese, I ate the cheese and the cracker, and he looked at Amelia. Her eyes held on his. Was it a doublecross?

He took Amelia's shoulder and slid his arm around her neck, and in a way leaned against her chest as he climbed to her ear, and cupping his hand by his mouth whispered to her, she made an outcry of fake surprise, laughed, and said, but

'Why?'

He looked around her cheek at me, and again whispered to her, and while I ate black caviar on an octagonal cracker she nodded, and said something I didn't catch, and Philip slid down and sat beside her and stuck his feet out over the edge of the sofa, and sighed.

'Well,' she said to him: 'Ask him.'

The boy shook his head, and glanced around the room locating cats; she sipped her drink and asked if I had a cigarette. I put my drink down and as I went in my pocket for the cigarettes, Philip watched me, and as I shook one out and offered it to her, he watched me, his eyes went from the cigarette to my face, from match being lit to the cigarette between her lips, and as flame and end of cigarette met, and the light caught, he was almost cross-eyed, and in my soft smile he blushed, glared at me in corrected vision, and as she exhaled he began to cough loudly, and wave away smoke with his hands. He rose from the sofa, and came to me, and stood in front of me between my foot crossed over my knee and the low table with all the food, and leaning over my leg taking a deep breath, coughed spit in my face whereupon, before he could gather his breath, I gave him a load of spit right back, and with a shriek he fell back almost into the celery bowl, eyes wide, and face bleached looking to mommy who was laughing, and in real fury turned his eyes on me, and whispered,

'*Shit!*'

and grabbed a long celery stalk, and smacked me on the

foot with it so the cheese stuffing popped out and fell on the floor, I caught the stalk, wrenched it from his hand and as he screaming wiggled away I laughed and smacked his ass with celery, the stalk broke, he got free and after slipping on the cheese on the floor leaped on the sofa and bounded across to the other side of Amelia, turned and looked at me, his eyes bright and his face crimson, he couldn't control it bursting into laughter, delighted, we all laughed, and the game was on. I smiled,

'Ready?'

'Yeah,' he grinned. But did he know? I glanced at Amelia, and she whispered something to him.

'Boss, man,' Philip chuckled, 'shit,' looked at her and went into such a personal laughter he began to shake, and as he shook and laughed she looked at me, smiling and slowly shaking her head—to say she would tell me later.

Screaming laughter, he pulled and grabbed his way up her body to her ear, and after whispering to her, drew back his head and looked at her seriously.

'Well,' she said, 'why don't you ask him?'

Again he peered around her cheek, a pretty nice cheek, and then he stood on the sofa beside her, and as he leaned back against the back of it she wiped cheese off the bottom of his bare foot with a paisley napkin as he laughed from the tickle with his hand on her shoulder he asked, as if honestly hoping, or something, Fielding? he asked, shyly,

'Will you play beanbag with me?'

'Sure.'

Amelia asked, 'Why not show him your new glove?'

My separation within all this closeness was too much, and I had the peculiar sense a certain force of amusement was on my side. Maybe it was the cats. Maybe they were watching him, saying, to me, Let's see you do to him what he does to us. A cat's bellylaugh to get me going, and Philip looked at me poignantly, and I had the feeling he was reading my mind.

'Do you like baseball?'

'Love it.'

'Do you play?'

'Yes.'

'For a team?'

I nodded.

'Who?'

'Max's Kansas City.'

His face changed, and he laughed in a way that meant he was angry to lose his anger, but the irony of it was too much, and in disbelief, he let go a short excited laugh—

'Kansas *City!*'

Amelia and I laughed with him, and I said, 'A restaurant. Not the city.'

He was angry immediately. I explained it. About a bar. Friends. Weekends. It embarrassed me a little, and Amelia said,

'But it isn't baseball, is it?'

'No,' I answered. 'Softball.'

'The name of the bar and restaurant is the name of the team,' she said to him.

'Who's Max,' Philip said.

'A poet, I said. 'It's pretty complicated.'

'Is it true?' Amelia laughed.

I answered yes and Philip looked at his mother. She didn't know any more about it than he did, she said, and he asked me where the team played, and I said in different fields across the city, and anticipated:

'Sunday afternoons,' and answered his look: 'Come whenever you want,' and he smiled, and asked,

'Would you like to see my baseball glove?'

Very much. Which I said.

And after he left the room to get it I said to her he was very sharp, she (naturally) nodded, and I said I respected the fact that after I had mentioned to him that she had told me he liked baseball, he had put the responsibility back on me—rightly, I felt—asking me if I really did like baseball.

There was a crash from the next room, and I looked at

her and she sipped her drink saying he was evidently angry because he couldn't find it.

'Did his father place responsibility as sharply?'

'Only on others, never on himself.'

'Then it's your judgment that's the influence,' I said. 'And I'm a hypocrite for my deduction—' I felt thin ice.

'Why?' she asked, startled.

Philip came into the room with his glove, and the rubber ball city kids use for stickball, they pronounce it Spaldeen, to them it's what Mays hits, Gibson throws, and Harrelson fields. But that ball is a baseball, made by Spaulding. But if a boy thinks he's Bob Gibson the rubber ball in his hand becomes a major-league item, and the street turns into Yankee Stadium.

I took Philip's Spaldeen and his glove, which he handed me—doubtful about me touching it—but allowed as Amelia gave him a sudden dark-eyed flash, he sighed a little, and let me take it from him, turned and faked a lunge at one of the cats racing under the loveseat by the window.

Red-cheeked Philip took a step toward the loveseat; the cat came out from underneath, jumped up on it and raced across and leaped to the back of a wing chair, onto the mantelpiece, across and took a long jump onto the back of the other wing chair, and from it tore across the wall of books clawing spines, made a wild leap into space, knocked over the floor lamp and sailed on a long angle down, hit and skidded along the floor at the foot of the wall with all the photographs, bounced off the front door, gathered itself and crept into the kitchen for a little drink of water. I put the glove on, shaking my head while Amelia and Philip picked up the floor lamp, and I punched the glove as another cat—glancelike and as hard to catch as a spring snowflake—melted from the room.

Philip laughed shrilly, and thumped his chest.

I finished my drink, and when she asked me if I wanted another I looked at her in such a thirsty way she laughed, and as she for a moment blurred, and then disappeared, reappeared, and with a look of love and laughter, vanished. Philip, catlike, watched me, and when I deliberately, and literally, didn't move a muscle, he walked across and looking at me, sat down not quite beside me, and with a sigh said,

'It's under the dining-room table.'

Something very clever and amusing caused me not to say what I wanted to, and when I heard her voice drift into the room,

'The beanbag's under the dining-room table, Philip, why don't you get it?'

I laughed.

His face went dark. Doublecrossed again.

Feeling like I was in somebody else's plot, I grinned, like old Happy Chandler, and said, 'Well, we all know.'

'Yeah, shit man,' he said, bitterly.

I flexed the leather fingers of the glove, a boy's glove, curving them around, and smacked into it hard. The leather was new and stiff and I suggested he get a can of neat's-foot oil, and rub it into the leather, work it in, and I saw that the thongs around the hand strap which lay across the back of the glove were loose, so I tightened them, tried it again, and decided it would be more securely against the back of his hand, and I looked up and he was looking at his glove on my hand, and as his eyes met mine I gave it to him.

'Try it on,' I said. 'I tightened that strap.'

He did, and I stood up, took his gloved hand in my left hand, and his bare right hand in my right hand, and telling him to make a fist, which he did, punched his fist into the pocket of the glove, it was funny, because he saw the difference right away, and looked up at Amelia as to himself,

'Boss man, *boss*.'

She leaned over and handed me my drink and her silk blouse opened, I saw one small naked breast and her eyes blazed.

'Hm?'

I can't wait / Neither can I

Philip smacked the glove, oblivious, and muttered boss man and I said I haven't heard that since the Army, and as she sat down and crossed her legs I looked at her legs, and then in her eyes, and on contact we winked, and sipped our drinks. I felt her body in my hands and my cock way up in her and her little red arrowhead sliding against my power and the sound of her voice in my ear as she came, writhing, my eyes must have shown it, for her eyes blurred, and slightly pleaded, pupils expanding, and facing each other we took a drink of our hard liquor.

I puffed my French cigarette—below the deadline, the tar and richness of the tobacco was delicious, and as it nearly burnt my fingers I put it out.

We munched some crackers, and she said why don't you two play catch while I see how the roast is coming?

Her light laugh floated around the room, and as she went away I heard her voice,

'Who knows? Maybe we can have one more drink—'

Ah, swell. I smiled, and felt her touch me.

Little did I know.

He took his position in the front hall, the front door directly behind him, and I stood under the arch of the entrance to the living room, I turned on the overhead light and threw the ball lightly to him, which he, hands frantic, lunged for and missed—he began to dance and scream and I smiled while he chased, hooted booted and knocked the ball around trying to pick it up, y'look like Charlie Chaplin, I laughed, in Amelia's laughter from the kitchen, and finally Philip got the ball, and threw it five feet over my head and I jumped, heavily, and missed, he made a shriek of victory echoing as I went into the living room and found it by the loveseat, and I walked back to my position and said O.K. try a little? and threw him a soft arc which, with one hand here and the other somewhere else, and both feet kicking the floor, he missed, and again chased around and finally got and as he threw he fell headlong against the gateleg on the folded dining table, making a terrific smash, and lay on the floor gasping laughter while I, his throw was so wild, almost knocked over the floor lamp, but I caught it, the lamp, and found the ball by the fireplace, and I went back to him and picked him up, hauled him ten feet closer to me so we were about that apart, and I threw him one in the way men throw to four-year-olds almost placing it in the glove, and he juggled it laughing, lost it, got it, bobbled it and then firmly caught it, and dropped it, and doubled over in laughter and kicked the ball by me into the living room and as I said what the hell is this, soccer? he screamed,

'SHIT!'

He lay on the floor in a fit of laughter, Amelia laughing in the kitchen, and I, having a feeling I was being taken, which I was, was going after and finding the ball under the sofa, exactly in front of the nose of a cat who gave me a positively disgusted look, Fuck off, man,

'sorry,' I said, rose with the ball, finished my drink, wiped my lips, had some caviar on a wheat thin, and returned to action. I helped Philip to his feet, he went rubbery-leg, and started skating, and fell down again, gasping shit oh shit

'Boss shit!' he cried, and I released him, he yelled loud and clear and fell on the floor completely, rolled over on his back yelling and laughing as Amelia, drinks in hand floated out of the kitchen smiling and gave me my drink as I grinned realizing it was a clean glass, and we went into the living room and sat down and sipped our drinks, and I lit a cigarette.

I said softly, 'Wow, is it always like this?'

'*It!*' she cried, indignantly. '*It!* It's *you!*'

'Got it,' I nodded. Oh boy.

Little Indian stood before me breathing hard, and for a moment, I—fuck it, I thought. Future tells.

'Play, catch,' he panted.

She had a way of making drinks *ice* cold, and as I stood, chewing on celery stuffed with cheddar, I took a long slug of the drink and stood up, took a drag off my smoke and handed it to her, and Philip and I returned to play catch. I gave him the ball.

He got about four feet away, and turned in a hate flash throwing the ball as hard as he could at me, and I caught it and lobbed it back to him. His hands came together naturally, as he was thinking about me catching that hard one, startled, and then he a little jumped, and missed it. So, he did have the idea, and I said,

'You do know. Keep your hands together. Let it come to you first, then bring your hands to it together. Don't jump at it.'

'O.K. O.K.,' he yelled, picked it up and threw, wildly, right at me. I caught it reaching to my left as it skimmed the tabletop, and said,

'Let it come to you. Use your glove. That's what it's for. Don't jump at it.'

He smacked his glove (me), and did a yeah-man-yeah dance, 'Boss shit,' and I threw an arc. Let it come to you.

He did and caught it. I congratulated him and said throw it to me, not at me, and as he began to stumble and laugh again, he ran at me and threw it in my face, a real Zen humor he had, and as I caught it, it made a hard *smack* against my palm, he fell sprawling forward and slid toward me in momentum, and stopped, face down on the floor at my feet, one arm under him and the other outflung, his ass went up and down as he laughed and slid his feet around and I stepped over him, and standing above his feet, I fired a fast one and heard it hit his ass, he screamed, and slipped and slid and got to his feet as I got the ball and threw it so it hit his ass reasonably again, and he screamed and began to weep NO FAIR, YOU HURT!

'Bull SHIT!'

I tossed it sidearm, bouncing it off him again and he fled from me shouting and crying to Amelia. I ran after him and as he cleverly doubled back suddenly and went into the kitchen, I leaped, and caught his hand, and as I slid, and my body slammed against the front door I said,

'You wanted to hurt me.'

'NO FAIR, YOU'RE BIGGER!'

'Play catch then—'

'Shit catch,' he said, throwing his glove into the living room. His lower lip came out and he began to cry. 'I want to play beanbag.'

Tears filled his eyes. 'Mommy. Tell Fielding I want to play beanbag.'

'You tell him.'

His eyes acknowledged the doublecross in slits, and he made a thin smile tremble, as he wiped his eyes.

'Beanbag,' he said to me, and sniffled.

'So you can bean me with a bag instead of a ball, right?' I threw him my handkerchief and told him to blow his nose. He was laughing helplessly, and he blew his nose a big gooey blow and threw the hanky back, unfolded, and I picked it up, muttered 'Jesus, what a mess,' and as he doubled over in laughter, I folded it and put it in my pocket hearing Amelia laughing, and Philip was saying no, he just wanted to play beanbag, he worked up a couple of sobs, and but then gave up and sat on the floor in laughter —to bean me—and I said O.K. you bean me I bean you.

'No fair.' But he was laughing so hard he had to support himself, hand on the floor and head lowered, moving in his deep humor. I said,

'How come no fair? Big Indian no savvy your rules—'

He looked up at me, and began, 'We'll play catch with my bean—' but he couldn't finish, and collapsed on the floor in laughter, and as myself and Amelia were laughing, too, I left him there, gasping baseball beanball, beanbag shit, boss, and as I sat next to Amelia grinning, and taking a good slug, I said,

'Is shit a new word?'

She made a gesture of yes and no, and I lit her cigarette as he appeared before me. She said,

'There are certain rules.' I smiled,

'His.' He said,

'Beanbag.'

I said, 'Look.'

'No look,' he said. 'Beanbag.'

'Please,' he added, and gave me a choirboy smile.

I figured he was desperate, and Amelia said in a kind of a turquoise mystery, 'Philip.'

'Fielding,' he said with changed voice, 'will you play beanbag with me?'

'Sure,' and suddenly he was before me, his groin against my knees, the celery bowl behind him, the beanbag in his right fist. The bag was about four inches square and full of buckshot, and with an evil glitter in his eye his arm blurred, I ducked my head to my left, whipped up my right hand and caught it—he had moved, lightning fast, from the room, but she transported, and was standing under the arch, and standing I made a low sidearm throw that nicked the tips of celery stalks and caught him smack on his ass jolting him forward, full face into his mother's arms, she sidestepped, caught his shoulder with her left hand, bent over and spanked him, hard, sending him nearly into the air, beyond her, but she caught him by his collar, and holding him while he really shrieked, spanked him again once, very hard, spun him around and pointed.

'Enough and to bed.'

He cringed against the side of the arch, face drained of blood, and tear-stained eyes gazing up at her, lips pouting, whispered,

'No, *no no*, Mommy—' and the look he had, as he hung his head, and looked up from under at her, was a political masterpiece.

Her face was drawn and angry, and he continued looking up at her, and when she murmured sternly I saw a certain aura. Her back was to me, but his face was up and his eyes transfixed on hers.

'Beanbag,' he whispered.

'Beanbag catch,' she added.

'Beanbag catch,' he confirmed. 'Yeh.'

She walked by me—I had risen and retrieved the bean-bag—she didn't look at me, and then she was smoking a cigarette and reading a magazine, and I was holding the beanbag and looking at Philip, who reasonably said,

'Would you throw it to me, Fielding?'

I lightly arced it, and he caught it, hands jumping out, and I said Let it come to you, and he threw it to me and I threw it back and he caught it, threw it to me overhand, I caught it and threw it to him underhand saying Let it come to you, keep your hands together, he did and caught it pretty well and we kept it up for a while, and he got I thought much better, he could grasp the beanbag, and then in a peculiar sense I saw he had a face behind his face, and one of them, whichever one, knew how, and did, suddenly, toss me a wink. He was smiling and about to laugh.

'Whaddya say,' I said, tossing it to him. I winked at him.

'Boss,' he said, and amended, 'fun, I mean,' and as he threw it back he yawned. And grinned, and yawned.

Amelia said, 'Um hum, Fielding, why don't you come in and finish your drink? Supper's almost ready.'

Philip's face—or faces—knit together—and focused in his awareness of her awareness. He slowly vanished, and I turned, and he was standing before her, with a look I did and didn't understand.

'Can I watch TV?'

She returned his look: a ping-pong look.

'What's on?'

His face darkened, and he had to speak—I smiled to my-self as I joined them, and saw his jaws clamp, lips purse, and then he really *yawned*, his eyes blurred and his body fought sleep as he said he didn't know and rubbed his eyes.

She smiled. 'Watch for a little.'

He vanished and I finished my drink. She asked,

'Another, and then supper?'

I nodded, to her serious face. 'Yes, a short one. Wonder-ful.'

So we had another and talked and nibbled, while Philip watched TV, and when Amelia went in to see how he was doing he was asleep, on her bed in front of the set. She undressed him, put him into pajamas, and stood by while he sleepily brushed his teeth, and when he went into his room and got in bed, I sat in the living room and watched the cats arrange themselves for the night, she having fed them while Philip and I played catch, and I felt, as the cats dropped into sleep, and I remembered the special silent communion of Mother at bedside, as He slipped into sleep, and night, and rest, and the deeps beyond.

I helped her serve supper as we finished our drinks in the process. I lit the candles, and opened the good red wine. All rather dreamily. Quietly, with style; both of us beautifully drunk, and the meal was just wonderful.

Coffee, brandy, and full stomachs. She said I appeared thoughtful, and I said yes.

'A little thing.'

She was silent, watching me.

'Once in a game in high school a ball was hit at my face. It could have killed me. Baseball, not softball.'

'How did it happen?'

'I was pitching, and the batter hit the ball at my face, very hard and I was off balance, but I caught it.'

'Were you frightened?'

'Afterwards yes. But not in the action. In those days I was pretty good, and on one fathomless blue Missouri afternoon, with a high dusty sky, I was pitching with everything I had, I was always nervous before the games, but when I got going, I loved it. I really loved it, and I was good enough to act instinctively. There was a runner on first and third, one out, and I was pitching from the stretch keeping an eye on the runners, so I went into my motion and delivered. I threw my body into the pitch, so I was going forward with my right leg in the air, my body supported and pivoting on my left leg, and after I threw, my right hand was all the way down at my left ankle and my left glove hand was flung out behind me as the batter completed his swing, and hit it as it crossed the plate at his knees, my face was down, but looking straight into the catcher's glove and the ball came at the crack of the bat on that line, and as I whipped my glove around my left foot shoved me off the mound toward first base and I caught the ball where my face had been, and as I stumbled backward to first, I fired a hard low sidearm throw to third, doubling the runner off, we were out of the inning and I walked off the field to my cheering bench, and, well, later, went on to win the game.'

'And twenty years later his beanbag reminded you.'

I nodded, and she put her coffee on the low marble-topped table, and kissed me and ran one hand through my hair and with the other, as I stretched in the thrill, she unzipped my fly, whispering *stay, don't go, please—*

Sliding onto sheets I slipped in her, we embraced hearts hammering as I moved up in deeper she sighed, we were so close, and in such passionate peace it was as if we were actually a total self, just us, it, and hard and very high in the feel as we rode all the in and out, and in, and hotter and out, and hotter and hotter dripping as she moved her slick clitoris and cervix and contracting pulled and I went in and she rode up and I pulled outward and she rode down breathing deep, I in her deepest living room field savage starry darkness fuller and fuller hurtling through space as she gripped me and her whole body was in my hands we looped through night into a cosmic *wham*, sun blast on water, archaic stones. Green trees, earth scent, mossy banks, I saw.

I did a wingover into insect darkness, and stayed with her until I fell out too small, and pulled the sheet over us to cover our fall, remembering our cries, as we kissed and murmured, as we did, slip blissfully, in a little tumble into sleep, and then again darkness. Like the night before—I woke. She was crouched over me, putting the wine bottle on the bedside table by me, and putting my cigarettes on the table on her side, beside the two wine glasses, as I glanced at the clock-radio we had napped about half an hour, and she handed me a full and chilled glass of wine. Her lean belly was a few inches from my face as she then leaned over me, and her pubic hair brushed my shoulder. I ran my hand along her legs, caressed her ass, and her dark and dank and dripping hair and pussy, I embraced her waist and pulled her down to me and I kissed her belly, and I from underneath licked her pussy for the taste of all and she made a soft cry, put the wine bottle down, and held herself steady and I kissed her thighs, and she raised herself, and turning her body kissing me she curled down my chest and licked my belly, and slightly lying on me, as I ran my hand around her back, and put my left hand between her legs she was soaking wet and my fingers touched and stroked her clitoris and she took my rising cock altogether in her mouth, and into her throat smoothly, and fondled my balls, and her head was moving up and down with her hips, and then she rose and turned, our hearts hammering, she entered my arms and we lay perspiring and kissing completely with my cock in her as she pulled on it, and our wet selves were together, in our flowing fucking, flowing I came, heart wild in the burst, she moving her pussy in circles and whimpering and licking my neck, and as I contracted she covered me with caresses, and kisses, and my little pecker popped out, I laughed in the tickle, and she whispered in my ear, *the wine is chilled—so good—*

oh you're of me

yes and you me we are we

and others, the I God, the wine was so good, and the rich tobacco as we sat up in bed drinking, and smoking, in our self.

She said, 'He'll be in around four or five.'

I nodded. 'He has the idea anyway.'

She swallowed wine and murmured in her throat, yes. Well, I said, this will confirm it, but we're of it, so no need for fear.

'Are you afraid?'

'I used to be.'

'Then you are, a little.'

I looked at her. 'I'm thinking of him, I want a positive effect. I don't want to hurt him, and I'm a little—'

'Apprehensive how not to. Normal, I'd say.'
Thankyou, we said.

She looked at me point blank. The look, savage without expectation, brimming with knowing, power, and a smoking inner eye, which is why they named that inner fluid in the jug of vinegar *Mother*—the mother in the jug of manhood, revealing the first line of the Stevens poem—

I corked the bottle of wine (half full), and put it on my bedside table, she blew out the candles, and we embraced and kissed and caressed and stayed in touch, bodies close, and then separated, and I lay in darkness thinking of her look and feeling her fall into sleep. I turned so I was lying facing the windows, warmly watching the curtains drift in soft cool nightbreeze in the soft light of moon letting the consciousness of the envisioned Hudson River lull me to sleep, in a sense of vastness, as if I had lain like so before and written of a man who dreamed of distant cities found in an invisible glass, I had done so, there was the river, and I, young and old together as she and I, in a fight for the mysteriously familiar and yet unknown footsteps, my oncoming steps at the gateway of the dream, so softly, not steps, no, small paddings, and I without motion woke opening to a slit my left eye, and saw his figure standing inches away, I felt his soft hot breath as he stood silhouetted against moon panes gazing at me in unmoving stillness, and in his dim eye sockets I saw at first a spark and as it gathered I saw tiny fires, getting larger, burning out at me, and tiny white-orange circles radiated hatred, and then they dimmed, and silently he softly turned away, and I heard him move around the bed, and after a strange lake-surface silence, I heard his child-soft voice,

Mommy?

Mmm?

My eyes aimed along my listening, and she was asleep, Holy mackerel, I thought, she's talking in—Philip whispered,

I don't want him here.

Mnn nnn?

No. Do you?
Mmm hmmm.
Why?
Like 'im.
You do?
Mmmmalot.
More than me?
Never.
Mommy, do you love me?
Um hum all my heart.
Does he?
Umm nn nuy ytum hm—
Does he like me?
Said he did, mm.
Is he a liar?
Amelia laughed in her sleep. *Nnnuh unh.* (I nodded
yes.)
    'How do you know?'
    'Don't know, good 'un.'
    'Mommy?'
She cleared her throat. 'What.'
Philip, doubtfully. 'Mommy.'
    'Do you want to come in, or sleep in your own bed.'
    'Mommy—' he hesitated.
    'No. Mommy sleep.'
    'Will he play beanbag with—'
Amelia angry: 'Yes! Sleep!'
Philip's voice changed because he was smiling; the ploy.
'Mommy, is Fielding a good baseball player?'
    'Um I' *mmm nno, um.* 'What?'
    'Will he be here tomorrow?'
    'Mhope so.'
    'Mommy?'
Amelia woke up completely and said something to him,
and I saw the aura of his body being pulled in contradic-
tory ways, as by his will, and her rule.
    'Go into your room!'

'Aw mommy.'

'Then come in here—'

I heard a murmur, like large animals finding peace, and felt the bed move as Philip climbed in with her, and I heard him whisper,

'Mommy?'

She said, furiously: 'NO MOMMY: YOU SLEEP!'

I heard him murmur O.K. and sigh, and then there was silence. I rubbed my hand over my face, and whispered something like Jesus, boy, holy mackerel.

I slept.

The plane came down from the sky, leveled, hit, bounced and taxied toward me and stopped as the prop shuddered, and then was still, and my sister and the pilot got out laughing. I was terrifically excited, and as they came toward me I scooped up a hard grounder and threw to first for the out. By a mile, and they were talking to each other; he was congratulating her.

She had landed the plane.

Her face was flushed with pride, and her eyes sparkled. The pilot grinned and said to me,

'O.K. sport: your turn,' and to avoid showing my excitement I walked a little sloppily toward the plane.

My sister smiled, 'I'll be watching.'

Up there she had known me below, watching up! She *had* seen me! and as I got into the Cub, I was very proud.

I woke hearing little noises in the kitchen. Combination crockery and silverware, and a voice,

Is he up?

Go see, she said.

I heard a door open, and Philip came into view, saw me looking at him, and went away, reporting to her that my eyes were open but I wasn't up, and the door swung open, she glided across to me, and offered a small glass of tomato juice with salt and pepper and a squeeze of lemon, and a drop of vodka, and kissed me saying take a shower, breakfast's almost ready, and in the sunlight I drank my bloody little mary, and embraced Amelia's waist lifting her shirttail and kissing her belly, ran a hand up her miniskirt and lifting and pulling panty down, I saw the bright red tip of her clitoris, erect, and standing in her pubic hair, and I nuzzled it and in pussy with knuckles saying take a shower with me as she rubbed her pussy in my face and laughed she already had, and then I was sitting up, my feet on the floor and she had vanished into kitchen noises.

I put on my undershorts with difficulty because of the scale of my erection, and went into the bathroom and pissed and showered, and shaved with her razor. I looked O.K. I thought, and felt better because of the drink, so I dressed and went into the kitchen, and sat beside Philip at the table. He ignored me when I said good morning, when I cleared my throat and sipped the hot black coffee feeling the warmth of the day. I smiled.

Our eyes met. She:

'Want to go to the park?'

I said that would be swell, and she asked me how I liked my eggs and I told her and we ate in pleasant strangeness as I fixed the wheel on Philip's toy car, and had my second cup of coffee, took a trip to the john and later with Amelia and Philip, a small bat, a lightweight plastic ball and Philip's glove, and sections of the Sunday Sulzberger edition, we rode down the elevator, left the building saying hello to the doorman (Eddy), and went out onto the street, across Riverside Drive and down into the park where we found a grassy area, and while Philip climbed around in one of a small row of gnarled trees, Amelia read the Sunday book-review, and I leafed through the magazine section one eye on Philip and one hand on her thigh as she ran her hand through my hair we talked about Doris Lessing.

'Mommy!'

Philip was stuck, and she rose, breezed over, reached up and disentangled his right foot from the limb's crotch, kissed his ankle, and the curve of her body in flowing profile was beautiful, I thought I saw a soft glow around her, the sunlight coming down through the trees in the distance gave her uplifted face a Renaissance quality, and hearing her laughter I saw her eyes—her lips grazed mine and she was lying beside me reading the newspaper.

Listen to this.

I did, partly, and looking across the Hudson River, wondered how such an incredible person could have gotten such a raw deal. I thought of myself, too, and then of our self, and Philip's urgent cry put her in the tree with him and he was crying, and whimpering.

Can't get down, Mommy.

I went through the grass, and standing beneath the tree looked up her skirt to white bikini panty, the trees were small and I reached up and with both hands took him by the waist and lowered him to the ground. He shouldered me away and climbed back up as she jumped down and walked with me back to the spot where the newspaper lay, and we sat down and as I lit a cigarette Philip began to cry.

'Tell him to come down and we'll play some ball,' I said.

She did, and he a little angrily accepted. Face dark, and feet and fists anxious to kick and hit, he stood at bat under a taller tree that was home plate as I pitched. Amelia played outfield.

First base was a paper plate under a stone, and third was her sandals on the book-review section. I pitched and he swung and missed and threw the ball over my head where Amelia fielded and returned it. I pitched again and he swung and missed, and after a couple of more like that I went to him, told him to hold the bat high and when he swung to take a step forward with his left foot, and when I pitched again he did. He hit the ball to the right of Amelia and ran around bases while she chased and got the ball, threw it to me, I hollered and chased him as he fleeing shrieked I dove and tagged him, he tripped over my hand and fell and began to whimper and curse me, and Amelia came in, gave him his glove and said it was her bat. Philip trudged muttering to the outfield.

She stood in front of the tree trunk and held the bat high and looked at me seriously and I pitched, it was too low, she returned it to me and I watched her as she threw: pelvis, and arm, like a longbow, and as her left foot kicked, the ball arced to me. I caught it against sunlight shining through the trees, and threw her an inside pitch and she stepped into it and hit it over the book-review section. I yelled GET IT PHILIP and heard him scream. She was around first base heading wildly toward third, his throw to me was off and I got the ball beside first base as she headed around third laughing into home as I ran hard across, dove full length at her with a shout—and missed—heard her outcry I'M SAFE as she embraced the tree trunk, her forward momentum carrying her feet off the ground, she fell, and I was kneeling at her side as she sat up seeing where the bark had scraped her wrist. I licked her wrists as Philip yelled COME ON SHIT PLAY BALL. I helped her up putting my hand on her ass, saying we'll put some vitamin E on it when we get back and she nodded and I went to bat with the score Amelia 1, me and Philip nothing. Philip pitched the ball about ten feet to my right and above my head and I ran after it and hit it and she cried FOUL! OUT!

'*Out?*' I asked angrily. 'What is this out shit?'

We argued, she saying one foul was out, and I, that had I known I wouldn't have swung, there should be at least two, and Philip was disgusted and at bat, and I was pitching. He took a half a dozen swings, missing, I commented on it to Amelia and she said strikes were free, one foul is out, and Philip hit the next pitch down the third-base line, two bumps and the grass stopped it. I got it but he was safe at first. Amelia walked to the plate.

'I have no outfield,' I said.

'I too have problems,' she smiled, tightlipped, and I said I know a plot when I see one, and she requested I pitch the ball, and I did, and she hit it over my head, and when I got it and had started toward home I saw her running around third and in with Philip in her arms, they both touched the tree and were safe and it was Amelia 2, Philip 1, and me nothing, and it was my bat. Philip pitched and I hit the ball over his head, she fielded it on the grass and I was on third base, Philip was at bat and Amelia said softly, hit it to me sweetheart, and I argued loudly, don't do it! It's a con! he hit it to her right and she picked it up and came toward me, I running just ahead of her, and just short of the tree trunk I stopped and turned and said come and get me, and as she leaped I ran around to the other side of the tree and peeped around at her. She stood, with the ball in her hand, looking at me. She faked a move to the right, and jumped left, *vanished*, and appearing on my right tagged me out.

94

I fell on the grass in laughter. She stood above me smiling.

'There is no hope,' I said from the grass.

A cloud came across the sun, and she said remember, Fielding.

'Mommy doesn't play.'

'You're telling me,' I said, getting up and dusting my pants.

I was pitching, and it suddenly began to seriously cloud up, and get quite chilly, so we got the stuff together and headed back to her apartment, and as we crossed a rise she said she'd go shopping for food for lunch and Philip began to gripe and scream ice cream, and when she asked if he wanted the usual he screamed louder, and I realized ice-cream was either one or two words and he didn't know what kind, and the two syllables blended into one scream, and on the path which led up to the Drive, he suddenly began to cry, and choke, and broke free from her and sat, and then lay down on the asphalt path, weeping *I scream*, and what, I thought apprehensively, was going on.

Crying his guts out he looked up at her, and his face changed into a blood-red mask of hatred, she took a step toward him as he cursed and spit and foamed, she grabbed his hand, swept him up off the path and flashed by me, across Riverside Drive, and vanished into the apartment house, I heard an outcry, and I crossed to Eddy, who was gazing with parted lips into the building. I joined them in the elevator and when we got off he was kicking and spitting she threw open the apartment door and disappeared, I heard a thud and a crash, a door slammed shut. A muffled scream, and a terrific crash.

I glanced in the kitchen and she was making two vodka tonics, and as I drank, she said let him work it out.

Sure enough. One smash followed another, crashing along with shit in any tonal combination, and as we both cleaned up the living room and did the dishes, I looked at the door to his room, it was split down the middle, and she explained a

95

certain especially bad night. He had beaten the center of the door out from the inside—with his fists—and I heard a silence, a scraping and then a creak and a firm crunch, splintering of wood and a very heavy crack, and crash.

'His bed,' Amelia murmured, and we went into the kitchen and I helped her put away dishes, and as it began to rain we sat at the kitchen table drinking and smoking my French cigarettes and talking about Robert Creeley's new book of poems, *Pieces*, the cats came in and ate, I was aware of silence, and tranquility, the kitchen door swung open and Philip came in, face streaked with dirt and tears, yet clear-eyed. He said, Mommy,

'can I watch TV?'

'Sure.'

The set went on, and she stood up saying she was going out for some food, and bending to me, kissed me, and when she asked me to stay for supper I accepted, I'll work on my book tomorrow, and she put on a bright yellow slicker, boots, and a Captain's Courageous hat, and with a see-ya-later wink, went to market.

I went in and sat on the bed next to him, and we watched TV a while.

When she returned he had some vanilla fudge ice cream, and then he took a nap and she and I stripped kissing and caressed and began to blend into our self and my heart pounding almost beyond control, I said, feeling her become me, I her,

'Be me.'

She stood up on the bed arms out to steady herself, and made her hands down her belly like she was fat like me and then her hands above her head like she was tall like me, and she made her hands make her hair long as mine was, straight and flowing, and she made my turned-up nose, and as I, lit an invisible cigarette as I do and turned to me myself, looked down at me directly, and I said,

'I love you.'

I pushed my thighs out, and held out my arms as I came

to her in her sound, and we embraced, and began fucking.

We said it again, crossed over into the future, and I had orgasm, and felt a strange innocent power as I held her, even as my cock was little she gripped it and ground her teeth in my collarbone, moving her head from left to right and in a shudder cried release, and kissed me passionately, as a shaft of sunlight poured into the room, through the breaking clouds above the river, we lay in continuity along the line in self, which I so deeply loved, and always after, I enjoyed her covering us with a sheet we set the alarm and napped.

Philip had a hamburger, tomato salad and cream soda. Amelia and I had cheese, caviar, and champagne, laughing and listening to old Frank Sinatra records we got very very drunk.

Strange and beautiful, that night, again we became each other so easily, and lay close at first and talked, naked and high above the city we blended, clouds rolled across the sky and I felt I had gone to our farthest side, and her loving distances were mine, as mine were hers, and in our near unconsciousness we made love, or let our love make us, and in our unknowing the power rose, centering in on the spirit of the visionary clitoris against penis moving pulling contracting she gripped me and we both sighed and cried out softly, and we came, and as I, we, she suddenly moved, I opened my eyes, Philip was walking into the room, and advancing to the bed.

'Mommy?'

She vanished from beneath me, and I heard her fierce *get out*, his hurt response,

What is Fielding doing on top of you?

Fast shuffle of feet, a cry and slam of door. Words whispered I missed, and she came back in, and was in my arms heart pounding, breathing it's too soon for that. I put my arm around her and lay back in shock.

But, I whispered, if he asks, tell him.

Not yet.

To myself: *boy the words ring true, and what shall I do.* I answered: *if he asks, tell him we're making love, and if he asks further, tell him that's how it's done, and if he asks further, tell him everything.*

I had an idea. It is too soon, I said, because he doesn't know me, but he will, and when you think he knows and accepts me, because you'll know before I will, let me know, too, and if he asks, I'll tell him.

Yes, she said, that's good. But you'll know, and you can judge. You're great. But not yet, though. But I will. Thank you. But he's going to be angry until then. I know him.

One night at the end of the first week we spent together I went up to her apartment after work and she said she had a surprise for me, and after Philip condescended to say hello, she took me into her room, and going to the closet in the hall opposite the bathroom, she took out, and brought in, and handed me a beautiful white and blue and orange paisley Oriental silk bathrobe, with sash, and huge cuffs. Mandarin collar.

It was what I wore whenever I was there. I took off my street clothes and put on my great wild bathrobe, and at summer's end, I had a deep tan, and really looked terrific in it.

I woke, got a cup of coffee and went in the living room and sat next to Amelia who was doing a crossword puzzle. My gaze fell on the cats.

Aside from their lust for cheese and antipasto, they were, like mad children, obsessed with the desire to catch flies, and if a fly buzzed by—no matter the cats awake or asleep—regardless what Amelia or Philip or myself was doing—sensing the fly, cat ears twitched, heads snapped up, and hair stood on end, tails out, eyes wide as they leaped into the air, claws out, bodies whirling and tearing the air apart for the fly, and following chased it through the apartment, as the fly went out the window the cats almost did too, twelve stories, but they never went all the way, in fact braked at the last moment, and lay, gloomily and angrily, on the windowsill, gazing out over the city licking their whiskers and searching air patterns.

But they caught flies, too—and often—to amputate and mash around, they chewed 'em up, spat 'em out, and watched 'em die, and it seemed the cats—and the flies which survived—got to know each other, a little.

One night after Philip had gone to bed, Amelia and I were on the sofa, reading and correcting the proofs of my story. The black and gray cat lay asleep on a small marble-topped table in front of the fireplace between the two wing chairs, its nose near the corner edge, its eyes closed. Image of a sleeping pussycat.

A slight motion caught my eye. I saw a fly land, and start walking along the edge toward the cat. It passed the cat's tail, and continued on, passing the rear paw and leg, and didn't stop until it passed the front paw on which the cat's jaw rested, and just under the cat's nose, the fly stopped.

'Look,' I whispered, and pointed.

The fly looked up into the slow pulsing cavernous nostrils, and then at the cat's paws and claws, at the whiskers, stirring gently. The fly seemed to pause a bit, then did a little dance, fluffed its wings, kicked up its legs, shuffled around a little, then settled down for a good cleaning and rearranging; it began grooming its wings, legs, knees, antennae, etc., until everything was smoothed down and ready to go, and the fly glanced up at the cat again, and walked toward the end corner of the table. Just as it was about to take off it looked back, kicked up its legs, returned, walked around the cat's claws, looked up the cat's jaw, yes, all cat, and then the fly returned to the corner of the table, looked into space, scratched a little, and just as it took off it saw a monstrous laughing colossus, two as if one, blending, and blurred in the relative distances of the universe.

Someone had forgotten to flush the toilet. A turd curled against the bottom.

I found Philip in the kitchen, and at my request—hey c'mere—his blasé expression vanished under the power of his curiosity, so, a little divided, and not trusting me much, he rose, and followed me into the bathroom. I pointed at the turd.

'That's shit,' I said.

He curled his lip, mumbled about aw he knew that.

'Uh huh,' I said, 'but it's what they mean when they say shit.'

He chuckled, and so did I, and as I left, I said flush that shit down, would ya? He did, and laughing glanced at me suspiciously.

I sat beside Amelia on the sofa, and picked up the book I was reading—a biography of Ezra Pound—and Philip lounged into view, and standing beside the end table with the lamp, he glanced at dozing cats, climbed up on the sofa and leaned against Amelia. He cupped his hand to whisper. I heard him begin

'*Mommy*, Fielding said—'

and after extended whispering he leaned back and looked at her.

'It is,' she said. 'He's right. Yes. That's the word.'

One Saturday we went to the park again, as we often did.

It was a narrow rather amorphous hilly ribbon of green that ran between Riverside Drive and the West Side Highway. The Hudson flowed beyond.

The drive up the highway is impressive, heading toward the majestic sweep of the George Washington Bridge, and passing, on the way, the big ships at dock. I remember an afternoon with my friend Gregory Turner, driving uptown we saw the *Leonardo da Vinci* docked, side by side with the *Michelangelo*.

The day was really a lovely day, and in the space within the city it was as the past merged with the future, the way true emotion: the way way-ahead love crystallizes distance. Amelia brought her bicycle, and though a little distracted, she seemed with the day, and we three walked around, bought ice cream sticks and a popsicle for Philip, she thought she'd go for a ride, she said, and I, feeling like everybody, figured she wanted to be alone, and she got on the bike, and pedaled away.

Philip and I found a strange long matted grass area at the bottom of a hill covered with trees and bushes. Standing on top of the hill we could see the river, and helplessly and without guilt, I remembered Elisa Victoria, whom years before I had loved so wildly one blazing summer city weekend when the town had been ours. I had a lot of money from an advance, and the memory of us standing under the inlaid tile arch overlooking the yacht basin with that bewitching three-masted schooner at anchor, and the brilliant orange sun ball, huge and hovering over New Jersey and not a cloud in the early evening sky, and the taste of the cold, delicious sangría—was fantastic. And afterwards walking along West 72nd Street holding hands as she sang With A Little Help From My Friends, she had a beautiful voice, melodic, she was, fluidly splendid and young, juicy and passionate hot-blooded body, she loved grass, she had a great sense of humor, and of despair, she was angry, and tender and sensitive and when I bought her the lavender-striped skin-tight minisheath for her dusky flesh she laughed and wept with gratitude. She had loved to take and had loved to give, she was powerful and tender and she carried a pearl-handled twenty-two pistol, and was ever on guard. She was sensual and caused tumult in the streets, she had once been raped, and was little more than a girl and every bit a woman. As resilient and as tough as Nature herself, and the meaning of the Hudson River and the 79th Street Boat Basin for the rest of my life. The river had many memories for me, and it was fun to stand with Philip and gaze out into them.

'Let's play!' he cried.

We went down the hill toward Riverside Drive to the matted place below, rather mysterious it was, and a bit secluded from the paths, yet occasionally I raised my head, and saw beautiful very desirable Amelia on a rise against the sky, pedaling along on her bicycle.

I found two fair-sized somewhat straight sticks, a couple of pint-sized crumpled cardboard milk containers and in a sandy clearing I dug a hole with my heel and announced we were going to have a game of golf.

I paced off about twenty-five feet to the right, and the same to the left, explaining the rules.

Philip went first and hit the ball an incredible shot, landing about two feet from the cup. He was in in three, and I yelled Damn!

'Just wait,' I said.

I shot, and shot again, and on three landed about ten feet from the cup, topped the next one, gave the next one a better stroke, and on the next one I was in. I was getting the feel.

'You've taken the first round,' I announced. 'Ten rounds in the game,' and placed his ball on a different angle than before, as I did my own ball, and as he had won, he went first, and again got off to a good start, and made it in five. I made it in six, so he was two rounds ahead. I won the next, we tied on the next, and it was two to one with a tie, and I put my ball on top of the hill and his under the bush, he whimpered a little and Amelia bicycled into the area.

'Arnold Palmer's ahead!' I said, glancing.

'*Philip's* winning?' she grinned.

I squinted my eyes. 'Yeah.'

She kissed the top of his head murmuring good boy, and came to me and put her arm around my waist, as Philip shot excitedly. And missed—the ball.

'I missed!' he screamed, 'Go again,' I said, 'Does it count?' he cried, 'No,' I said, and he went and it skipped out a little, he said shit, and hit it again, and eleven strokes later he was in.

'How's the bike riding?' I asked her.

'Dull,' she said. 'I want us.'

We laughed ha ha uh huh yeah sure you bet right here.

Watch this. I made it down the hill and across in ten and on the next I was in, so Philip and I were even, with one tie, and Amelia asked how long this was going to continue, she wanted a popsicle, so Philip and I decided to play the final, and see who won.

I looked at him after his first shot. I was a little ill-tempered, and mentioned a little rat, and announced that my form was off today, and had I been on—well. But he typically rather ignored me. Mommy was back. Guess who won.

We found a Good Humor man, and after I'd made a couple of wisecracks about that, we walked along eating popsicles until we came to a little playground, and as other kids Philip's age played under an overhead sprinkler, Amelia suggested he take off his shoes and socks and shirt and play in the water with them, and he did and he was fun to watch. She lay on a bench and got some sun, I sat and smoked and watched him, and I thought he was pretty good.

He got along O.K. No fighting, and fair in sharing the spray. There wasn't room for more than three or four, and I thought that what he liked was the other kids around him, he had an ego-expression I liked, and occasionally he glanced at me, to look away to Amelia immediately, and a few minutes later came and stood in front of me as if when things were going the way he liked, and Amelia was asleep, or not there, he could tolerate me.

'Fielding,' he said quietly. 'Stand under the water.'

I rose, and went and stood under the water. The kids all laughed and shouted and pointed, as I smiled, Lookie lookie, The Man In The Shower With All His Clothes On! getting soaked, while Philip shook with laughter, saying Mommy, look at Fielding! and she sat up and looked at me and grinned shaking her head from side to side, 'He'll do anything for a little attention.'

'But I told him to,' Philip said.

'And he did?'

Philip pointed at me, yeh—him—and as the shower had been rigged for small children, I felt like an elephant in the bathtub, watching the other animals watching me.

Tough, Amelia chuckled, *but oh so gentle.*

Watch it, I warned, *that'll date you—*

Remember that ad from the forties?

She said she was going to take her vacation in August. She and Philip were going to England, and as I had mine set up at my job for the last two weeks of August, it meant we wouldn't see each other until September, and she began mentioning England, occasionally, and around the second week in July she began to get that look in her eye, about things being put into suitcases, and her businesswoman's mind began, very objectively, getting all her things packed, letters written, and the apartment in order. I heard it in her voice, and as we were in the habit of talking like each other, I heard myself in her voice, using my punctuation, talking about this going there and, that— maybe later.

Will I need it?

'Think about it,' I said. 'You've got three weeks.'

'The maid's coming next Friday,' she said.

'Maid?'

'To give this place a good cleaning.'

'Yeah, a good cleaning,' I said, and joked, 'a maid hasn't given an apartment a good cleaning in one hundred years. Slavery is over. Where have you been?'

'I pay her—'

'Because you're a capitalist brought up, however anxiously, by capitalists. She do a good job?'

'No, and I suppose you're right. Why should she.'

I nodded. 'Do it yourself. Or let me.'

'You?' she laughed.

'Sure, the slaves are free, so are the women, and so am I. Free, literally. Think about it.'

'How can I fire her?' Amelia laughed.

'How can you hire her?'

'The last one stole my jewelry.'

'Did you need jewelry?'

'You're being hostile,' she said angrily, and I said I was angry and sarcastic because she didn't need a maid at all. 'It's a throwback,' I said, 'you're playing the role of your mother.'

She gave me a speech about how the maid comes before the big holidays and vacations to clean the place up, that's all, that she, Amelia, was sick of cleaning all year, and would willingly pay someone to do it, and what was wrong with that, to simply pay some one to do it. Besides, the woman needed money anyway and was grateful enough although, she admitted, it was, she supposed, wrong, the maid was a black woman, and was like Amelia herself, lazy, hated to clean, and furthermore, she, Amelia, was aware she had been playing a role from her past, but she couldn't help it, and to hell with it the maid was coming next Friday, case closed.

'That maid gets finished here,' I said, 'send her down to City Hall, I hear it needs cleaning up too.'

'Very corny and funny. Ha ha,' she said, like me. 'Also irrational,' she added. Like her.

I, with the help of an invisible cane, made my way to the wing chair, sat down, sighed, unfolded an invisible newspaper, tugged on an invisible vest, crossed my legs and puffed on an invisible cigar, and glanced at her like the man in the straw hat in the center of the photograph—her dead father. 'I thought you said she needed work.'

We laughed at me, and I said I was going to miss her, and she said I'd get a lot of work done while she was away, and then she asked me about yesterday—I'd spent the afternoon and night downtown in my loft writing—and I said an amusing thing happened. It had been a warm but drizzly day, and I turned back into my self to tell her. But first, as a bottle of opened cool wine was in my hands, I asked for a bottle of—I filled two glasses while she chuckled, and curled up on the floor at my feet, and as she lay her arm across my knees, and her chin on her arm, I stroked her hair, and saw a long look in her eyes in her upturned face.

'I'll miss you too. Will you write?'

'Of course. Let me know your address.'

Yesterday, you'll remember, was warm and drizzly, and I was perspiring in my good old dirty cream-colored raincoat. I needed a shave, was a little drunk, and after I had gone into Bohack's Supermarket and filled my basket with the basics, and went to stand in line, I saw the store was jammed with customers, and the lines wavered as patient and impatient men and women made way for others to pass with their shopping baskets on wheels loaded with food and babies.

Young men and women worked the cash registers, crash registers, two Oriental girls, several black men, and a couple of white men and boys all filled bags—managers and help alike—friendly, smiling, and fast, but instead of diminishing the lines, the lines grew longer because more people were coming in and I glanced at the tide hearing cars and trucks and taxis complaining up and down Third Avenue in their rush-hour racket, and I glanced behind me as I felt a bump against my ass. A lean, pimply kid apologized, I said O.K., and stood there patiently sweating, holding my heavy hand basket of meat and corn and vegetables and fruit and coming into view on my right I saw a black woman bending over a small black boy in the entrance to an aisle, she and he were face to face, happily singing the words to the tune of the canned song, On The Street Where You Live coming over the store loudspeakers. She had a great vibrato, and her face was familiar—it was Thelma Carpenter! and when the song was over, they held hands and continued walking as a white supermarket cop came around a corner and said to nobody,

'I thought the Grand Union was a bag, but *this*, Jesus—*Je-whiz!*'

And went his way with a big grin.

I inched toward, and reached, the big vertical rack of popcorn, potato chips, corn chips, Oreo cookie chewing gum Hersheybar M&M session, and way across the store to my left I saw an ancient, pouch-shaped Indo-European woman in torn and dirty calico rags and a gunnysack shawl walking as through deep water, struggling through cosmic currents across the store toward the cash registers, holding—gripping—a large grapefruit, and talking to herself, and the grapefruit smiling and frowning in her reactions, and looking at all the people, the old woman caught the eye of the manager at the first register, and she lifted her raisin-textured field-raked skull, white hair streaming, and yelled in a gummy toothless husky accent,

'HAH! I LOVE BOHACK'S!'

Managers, boys and girls and customers began to laugh, but—but not like the old woman. She was coughing and leering and laughing and repeating a phlegmy hah HAH her pinched eyes lost in wrinkles as someone let her in line, and as she stepped in she looked up at the ceiling, and yelled,

'HEY HAH I *LOVE* EVERYBODY SHOP BOHACK!'

She shuffled to the register unwrapping a worn and crummy scrap of cheesecloth under the eye of the smiling black manager, and she scrounged around and came up with twenty-one cents, paid him, and shuffled out.

So, in my line it finally came my turn, and I piled the food on the runway as the short Jewish man with the name ABE penciled on a card buttoned to his white butcher's jacket rang it up and put my food in a bag and wished me a pleasant weekend—I, startled, my appearance, I laughed and thanked and paid him, swept the bag of groceries into my arms and followed the swinging door out onto 18th

Street, where I turned left and headed toward my loft to work on my book. I saw the old woman sitting on a fireplug that projected from the wall of the new apartment house. She was counting the pennies in her cheesecloth rag, the grapefruit was almost lost in the folds in her lap, and as I walked by she raised her head, looked at me, and as she always does, for I've seen her often in my neighborhood, she hangs around hotels and laundries, supermarkets and subway stations. She nodded and grinned through a thousand wrinkles, rasped hello, and after I'd smiled and waved in return, and walked a few feet ahead, I looked back. She had her head down, no more grin, she was as serious as Bess Meyerson, counting her change in that filthy cheesecloth rag.

I paused and looked at Amelia. She nodded, and said I was a born storyteller, and I said all right, listen to this:

'One day a few years ago before I could love myself— before I met you—on a beautiful cool October afternoon, shaved and spotless in my brand-new cream-colored raincoat, I crossed Lexington Avenue and headed down toward the Gramercy Hotel. I saw, then—again, for she'd always been in my neighborhood—the old lady of the field (the storyline is the field,' I remarked. 'Of energy,' Amelia added, and sipped wine as I nodded)—'sitting on the edge of the concrete-rimmed shrub area outside the hotel dining-room windows, flicker of waiters and wealthy people inside, eating and drinking, and as I grinned hello to the old lady she threw a big wave of the hand to me, and as I passed her, she reached out at my raincoat, and I stopped, and took a couple of steps back. She took firm hold of my coattail, and looking up at me frowned, and expressed awe, then puzzlement, and then disbelief, and on the certification it was who she thought it was, she let go a good long bawdy laugh, and her happiness became the wrinkled mask of her face, and her dark and beady old eyes sparkled as she confided to me in a voice like a hoe striking a rock, did I know what I looked like? No, I said, A movie star, she grinned, and then made a choke cackle-cough, and rocked back and forth in phlegmy self-laughter, and suddenly lurching forward, she dropped the laugh, she gravely shook her parsnip-colored fist at me, and growled *you do, yah, you do!'*

'Indeed you do,' Amelia smiled, handing me her empty wine glass.

She put the book down.

'Where is Fielding?' she asked.

Then he called to say he would be late. He had picked up his mail, and was downtown answering letters. *I hear Mozart.*

Philip was in a nasty mood. He had gotten into a scuffle with some big guys at the playground, and was in his room, door closed, wouldn't speak to her. She heard him tearing up his room.

She washed her panties, the blue cotton blouse Fielding liked, and she made herself a drink as she made Philip's supper—he didn't eat much of it, and afterward watched television. At seven-thirty she put him in the tub, and washed him and then let him play, but he was very angry, his body was rigid, and his eyes were brimming with tears, and urge of release.

She was putting makeup on as the doorbell rang, she swept open the door and they kissed, and Fielding followed her into the kitchen and she made a couple of stiff drinks as he kissed her neck, and while they sipped and talked, she began making supper.

Then she came into my arms.

'What's wrong.'

'Philip's really furious. He got in a fight with some big guys in the playground.'

'Those bastards,' I said, and held her, and she snuggled close to me. I kissed her ear, and said, I'm sorry. Then I said, 'Not only have you become me, but my new book, too. Ever have a Lesbian affair?'

'Nnnnh,' she murmured.

'Ever thought of it?'

She shook her head and I asked her about with her sister, no, and she said she envied her sister's big breasts, and I said if it were the other way around she'd envy her sister's small breasts, forget it, I said, and as if her sister were mine I felt an old incestuous pull, I had tried all I could to feel my sister—up, and down if possible, and I asked Amelia if her sister had wanted to make it with her.

She frowned. Maybe. 'Could be.'

'Well,' I said, 'this us becoming each other raises the homosexual angle, and I just wondered. Incest, too. Who's between us and mother? Sister. A complicated repression,' and I thought about that, and then added,

'My new book begins with my sister and I, but I'm keep-it low key, doing it by tone instead of analysis, and swinging around us, Philip, and baseball. Straight Mozart.'

She said, in a low menacing voice, 'You heard nothing of what I said. You're so Goddamned self-involved, and manip-ulative we only exist after the fact—'

'I'm sorry,' I said. 'I have to do it.'

I heard Philip in the tub—she had awakened me—smash-ing the water, making geysers, and cursing. She put cloves in the ham and asked me if I ever had any sex with men, and I said yes, that I'd written about it, and when she asked if it had worked, I said seldom, and that I'd considered myself lucky.

Lucky, she repeated.

I nodded. When it was good, it was good.

'Mostly it wasn't?'

'Right.' Terrific crash in the bathroom, followed by two fast smashing, hammering sounds I couldn't identify,

'Why?' she asked alarmed, and disappeared.

'Because I wanted to—felt I had to,' I said to myself.

I heard him scream and curse her, and then a sound that caused me to move quickly into the bathroom. I saw Amelia standing with her back and hands flat against the wall looking down at him in the tub. He had a bowling pin raised over his head, and he threw it against the baked enamel rear of the tub. It crashed against it, bounced up off against the tiled wall, and splashed into his lap where he grabbed it, Amelia seemed transfixed, her eyes staring. Philip's face was lined redly and with a stifled scream he threw the pin again, and as it ricocheted off the tub, a terrible sound, and he was reaching for it, it was spinning toward him, I caught it in front of his face, it was a professional tenpin, weighed at least three pounds, was *hard* wood, and as he stood up and began to scream and demand it, I said nothing doing.

Something was wrong. She looked at me pleading, and I moved fast: he was out of her hands, he could go too far, and had gone too far. Beyond her. I swept him out of the tub and whipped a large towel around his body, he swung at me and just missed, had he hit my nose he would have broken it, tough kid, writhing in my hands, I held him by both muscles, his feet got tangled in the towel and I took him into the living room as he threw back his head to gather breath to scream, the veins bulging in his neck and temples, and he *screamed*, and shrieked and spit on me as I held him as Amelia began wiping up the puddled bathroom floor, I said to him straightly, if you break that tub you'll create a problem you can't comprehend, and I held him strongly. My face to his, his arms pinned to his sides in the towel, his face contorted, my face blank, grim, in fact, and I let him shout it out.

Cruel of me. He threw his head from side to side; wept deep and bitter tears, and had he the means he would have murdered me without mercy. I felt his power, his heart was strong and his fevered blood was held by strong veins and arteries, he was a terrific organism, and slowly I sensed his rage diminish, and I a little loosened my grip. He spit in my face and cursed and choked and bared his teeth, and suddenly hung his head, panting with exhaustion, and wept.

'Philip,' I said.

His foot lashed out and kicked me on my shin, and the pain his bare toe suffered sent him into a paroxysm, a black Oz of fury, he went absolutely savage, howled and twisted and spit and cursed, with everything he had. He was the distillation of pure emotion, and with his eyes bulged, slashed verbal anathema:

'*You're not my father.*'

God I felt sad and sick, *You're not my son*, and kept silent, and held him until I felt his body, altogether against his will, gradually relax, and as he whimpered I held him so he wouldn't collapse, and I unwound the towel and dried him, he let me, as he sniffled and yawned, and when he was dry I picked him up and took him into his room, and put him on his feet by his bed. He leaned against it, and said,

'Go way. I want Mommy.'

'She's yours,' I said softly, and left the room as Amelia came in.

I went in the kitchen, finished my drink and made another, checked the ham, and sat at the table a little glassy-eyed and read some of that Sulzberger shit until she returned. She ran her hand through my hair, knelt before me, put her head on my knees, and embraced my legs.

I leaned forward, held her head in my hands, and kissed her hair, and laid my cheek there. We stayed like that a while.

One Sunday afternoon, like lines from Eliot,

> 'When Mr. Apollinax visited the United States
> His laughter tinkled among the teacups.'

Mister and Missus Tarragon Chutney with their son Basil and daughter Coriander came to Amelia's apartment for tea, and the first thing being asked was how we were, and we were fine, great in fact, so were they, they said doubtfully, and we took their coats and hats and sat in the living room; where was Philip? At camp for the weekend, I said. *Well,* Missus Chutney said, Basil and Corie are in summer school, and doing fine, and it's good to have them with us. Corie's going to major in psychology.

When she gets to college, I said. Amelia smiled.

Of course, Missus Chutney said. I thought: I generally feel angry when you visit, because you are so uselessly rich. Actually we hate them.

Basil asked if he could turn the television on, and I said sure, so he turned the knob and the picture came on like wings (fluttering), and he said it didn't seem to work.

Give it a chance, his father said: an industrialist.

I said it wasn't a very good set, and Basil said ours is in color, and I said we hadn't thought to buy one in color, and he asked why, and I said we hadn't thought to buy one in color, and he asked why, and I said we don't like TV in color, and only watch the news in black and white plus an occasional movie, and Mannix, and he asked, and I watched his eyes as he spoke I wondered how he would react if I thought to kill him: you, by da troat. Could he read me? Actually, I rather liked him.

Don't you like sports?

We love sports, Amelia said. Especially baseball.

Live, I added. Not on television.

Oh, yeah he said childishly, and a picture came on, wavered, and disappeared, and he fiddled with the knobs and everybody watched him.

Amelia went over and as the image began to roll, she gave it a hard smack on top and the machine went through a reaction, blanked out, went on, fizzled, snowed, went black, and suddenly came clear and a man was talking about how to cut carrots with a French knife.

Sunday afternoon television. But he was right. I catch those things. I was a cook in the Army, I said. He's right, and I pointed to the TV set.

She looked at me, and I smiled *just a little*; No, I said out loud, I'm not doing it again! They all blinked. You use a French knife for cutting carrots; it's a fact. Trim 'em, line 'em up and knock 'em off crosswise.

Who wants to watch a cook, Basil said.

Change the station, Coriander said.

It'll go on the blink, again.

Hit it, Amelia said.

Basil grinned, and switched to another channel, and the machine went funny again, he hit it and it went blank and stayed blank, and as Amelia crossed the room to it she asked Coriander why she was interested in psychology.

At such an early age.

Amelia smacked the TV set, nothing happened and she tapped it four rapid shots, and it went on and several men in scant clothing chased a large ball around a wooden floor, and Basil asked me if I liked basketball.

Sure, I said.

But not on TV, he said.

I nodded, and Coriander said in between that, it was, had been, rather, her mother's idea, and Amelia affected surprise, and looked at Missus Chutney, and cocked an eyebrow.

Well, Missus Chutney said, I thought, well, Corie's such an introspective girl, and at such an early age, I thought if she could get an interest up, everybody's interested in psychology, and

Are you?

Why certainly. Aren't you?

Amelia grinned and I laughed yes, Basil said boy, *wow*, gee, etc., and Mister Chutney lit a menthol, a one hundred, and sighed.

I thought you had been involved, Missus Chutney said. She used to be, I said.

Amelia glanced at me and in the kitchen the little gizmo on the kettle began to whistle, and she went into the kitchen and when it petered out I said she had been in the old days, before books, a psychologist, and I asked, queried rather, hadn't that been the cause of their meeting?

Chutney, himself, looked at me. Hisself, I thought, oh fuck you, but my eyes had that funny just-opened surprised look it's fun to have on, and he asked,

You mean Corie?

I thought it was maybe for Corie and Basil, I said. Oh, I added, you mean psychology.

Basil? the Missus said; and I laughed yes, Basil. Hi Baz, he's over there watching television, the Knicks, in fact. I jerked my thumb.

Well really, the Missus said.

Well, I thought it was. Weren't you trying to find a school for them when you and Pepper met?

I like psychology O.K., Coriander said.

Me too, I said. Live, not on television, and I grinned. The race was about to start.

I can laugh in a weird way when I want.

Amelia came in with the tea.

Pepper! exclaimed Missus Chutney: BROWNIES!

And suddenly I had the image of Rumpelstiltskin, coming out through the wallpaper compulsively eating brownies, stuffing his mouth with their bodies, blood running down his chin and hands and the wall.

Boy! Did you see that? Basil asked me.

I made a sound in my throat and said I sure did. Did you?

Amelia poured tea and laughed: He was watching something else, and she gave me her witch's glance, and for an intuitive second lines crossed, and Mister and Missus Chutney began mouthing brownies and dropping crumbs all over the place. Amelia took a couple, with a cup of tea, to Basil, who sipped and ate and watched the Knicks. Bimbam. Pow: basket!

Frazier.

Mister Chutney put out the cigarette, and I had the feeling I wanted something *strrrange* to happen, like in a novel, and a voice said forget it. Look in the mirror.

I laughed, and brightened, and asked, tuning in to Amelia, I had thought you met Pepper—I said this to Missus Chutney—I thought you met Pepper when you were looking for a school for Basil and Coriander to go to.

True, Missus Chutney said.

Then where are we?

Must you *always!* question the obvious? Amelia asked me.

For answers, I said. Hey—wait a second, I added, and then I said oh—

realizing when Missus Chutney met Amelia—she called her Pepper (spirit)—in the detergent ad on television (before books) Missus Chutney had said she was trying to find a school for her brilliant son and daughter and in that way the two women had become sort of friends, and Amelia had found a school and everything worked out O.K., and the friendship sort of continued, and they visited us occasionally, and here they were. I often wondered if she had the hots for Amelia, could be, as actually Amelia hates the Missus pretty murderously—which the Missus might like. Then I thought I oughta get my mind off sex, especially in this surface.

The kids were interesting, though. They had a lizard quality, moving in their own directions leaving their little threadlike spoors.

I said, I'm glad Pepper had a good influence on you; to the Missus.

Who said, What do you mean?

I asked, Are you asking me what I meant?

She blushed, and I asked, Isn't that what caused you to think of Corie studying psychology, you meeting Pepper on that TV ad?

Amelia looked at me furiously. For Christ's sake, she said.

Well, you were a psychologist then, I said angrily, and Mister Chutney laughed and choked on a brownie. I was angry: Then what the hell is this about?

What is *what* about, Amelia snarled. Goddammit, you're impossible. You *are!* You're so dense, overcomplicated and —selfish.

I stood up and pointed at her: You tell me what's going on here. I don't know.

How do I know? I was making tea.

Nobody makes tea, I said. It makes itself. Tell me.

I sat down as she looked at me. No: *I'm following.* That was me.

Her eyes changed, and she nodded, and said, What he means, Marge, is he thinks I had some kind of influence on your decision and/or interest in both your and Corie's involvement in psychology, and knowing him, he'll next want to know if it's true.

She made a tight smile.

I can't call her Marge. Can't bear it—that's me thinking.

The Missus smiled, and said, head lowered, Well, it's
probably true.

Swell, I grinned, and how does Corie feel about it?

Corie?

Yeah, I pointed—Corie over there. Remember Corie?
and Corie answered,

I like it but I don't know if I'll make a career out of it.

Amelia and I smiled, simultaneously: Don't.

But the Missus Chutney, as Amelia and I laughed a ha
ha in knowing what would come next—

WHY?

Psychology is for children to know, Amelia said—which
is WHAT? cried the Missus—like money was for the
Dodgers to want—which was WHAT? cried the Missus—
and you mean in Brooklyn? Yes, answered Amelia, it did
nothing, but make them move to a different place.

Los Angeles, Basil said.

Holy smoke, let's go, Corie laughed.

The sun was going down over the town and Mister Chutney gave me that what-do-you-have-to-drink look, and added,

What are you writing?

I smiled, Some cheap Scotch, vodka, and some pretty good gin, and the book that will give me the money to reject the Nobel Prize they forgot to offer on my last one.

Do you have any vermouth?

I frowned, and Amelia said she thought so, crossed the room and opened the door of the cabinet. The hinge was broken, but to impress ourselves that it works, there's a way we do it. She opened the door, looked in and there was a little vermouth.

He lit another menthol one hundred and asked if he could have a small, dry martini, with an olive.

With a twist of lemon, I answered him. We don't have any olives.

No olives? Fine, he said, and I stood up and went to the cabinet and Amelia handed me the booze and I went in the kitchen and made his drink, plus two vodka tonics for myself and Amelia. Missus C didn't drink.

Here we go, I said, handing the Mister his, and crossing to my chair, I glanced down at Basil, who was looking up at me. You O.K.?

O.K., he smiled socially. Our eyes met.

Are you? I tested.

His eyes contracted in the effort. Blocked, well no wonder.

I sat down and sipped my drink, and the Mister Chutney stared into space. Sipping. Um! he exclaimed.

Funny, isn't he, I thought. So poor. V*erde, verde*, I thought.

He glanced at me, so he must have caught something. What's the book about? he asked.

A love story, I said.

He expressed a response, and a rather lonely warmth came into his eyes. Really?

Yes, I said, and we sipped our drinks.

Is it true?

True indeed.

Amelia and the Missus were going over a skirt pattern. Vogue Pattern Book. Coriander rose and sat by her brother on the floor in front of the television set.

She put her arm over his shoulder and he put his arm around her waist and they sipped tea and nibbled brownie crumbs, grinding loose nuts between their jaws, and talking about the game. I was reading the Mister's head, him wondering where I'd gotten true material for a love story— enough to write a *book!* But—a novel?

He sipped again, and said,

This is very good, but um, when you say a true

I said, This past Thanksgiving Pepper and I both made dinner, and as I was going through her cookbook, with the turkey cookin' and the good drinks and the smells and the way she was beside me—

So it's about her!

Yes, I lied of necessity, and said I had been rereading Dashiell Hammett's novel *The Thin Man.* It's been an influence, I said, as all his writing has, and as she and I made our Thanksgiving dinner, things came together within, and as I read and reread the spice labels—the ingredients— nouns like salt, sugar, etc., I saw a potential story—

Ah, he said. Therefore—

Exactly, I said, and we sipped our drinks.

You're violating
I looked at her easily and shook my head. Not me.
Don't
I'm following
How—what
The storyline
To where
Its own end—our future. Watching the kids?
I'm watching you
Give it up and so I clued him; why not
I love you, don't give it away
Never

A science, he murmured.

I mumbled, um hum, but for Corie?

Corie? he said.

I jerked my thumb and said yeah, she's over
and I sneered for Christ's sake. He looked at me angrily.
Silent. Science, she said. What's wrong with science?

Amelia buzzed me. Well, I said, she's thirteen years old
and has an interest in psychology or better a curiosity, and
not about science, but, probably about the power, and without going through it all again, how do you feel about that?

He looked at me; feel?

I grinned. Power.

No! Not like that!

I nodded O.K. and glanced at her; temptation, it was,
hones' and Well, he said, if she likes it, and Marge likes it,
it's O.K. by me.

Whadda hell, I muttered. Kalamazoo and jelly beans.
Zzzzzip!

Hm?

Amelia said, in a voice that could crush glass, Go: heat
some more water.

I went in the kitchen, drank a slug of vodka from the
bottle, filled and put the kettle over the flame, and as I
turned to leave, Mister Chutney stood in the doorway, glass
in hand.

I'm sorry, he said. Curiosity is fine. May I have another?

Absolutely, I said, and took his glass, and made him another; running a thin piece of lemon peel around the rim and dropping it in. It was a good drink, and ice cold.

You do it very well.

I smiled. The best are made at home.

He mentioned the name of a restaurant, something about a poet named Max—I'd heard of it, and even eaten there—and he said the day man made good drinks. I agreed. Frank.

He said, Maybe it's because everything you use at home is your own.

I nodded, having thought of that, and said, the whole action is subjective and thought *big fuckin'deal.*

I poured vodka over ice, added a lemon peel for me, handed him his, and taking mine with me, we returned to the living room.

Actually, he whispered on the way, I don't give a damn about psychology, and Corie's much too young for that stuff anyway.

Don't you want to go to a different place? I joked, grinned, put my hand on his shoulder, and looked at him warmly, saying under my breath, Whaddya wanna bet she agrees?

He tilted his head back and laughed; a grimace. Yes, he said, yes, and of that power stuff—

It's her brother, I chuckled.

Chutney cried NO! and Coriander looked up saying I'm bored, let's go home and play rummy.

Later, he said. Dear.

I asked Basil, What do you think about psychology?

I think it stinks, and so does Corie.

I don't! she cried, putting her hand over his mouth: shh.

He broke free, and loudly: THAT'S NOT WHAT YOU TOLD ME!

You're hopeless
A little, I laughed.

In twilight the industrialist's big car rolled silently down Riverside Drive. They were gone.

I took a nap, and had a dream

I dreamed I was everybody

Nibbling fresh asparagus by candlelight with wine. Philip was asleep.

'I've something funny to tell you,' I grinned, and she made a *tell me* smile.

'I saw Chutney yesterday. We had a drink at Max's. He was a little loaded, and as we talked we noticed a businessman we both knew, and I told Chutney the fellow was queer.

Impossible! cried Chutney.

'Not at all,' I smiled, 'and, in fact, if you'd check closer, watch his behavior, you'd see he's as fruity as a—'

'I can't listen,' Chutney said.

'O.K.,' I said, and I gestured to Frank, the bartender, 'we'll have two—'

No no, I insist, Chutney insisted.

I thought of Thackeray, in *Henry Esmond*, describing a woman: 'lean and yellow and long of the tooth,' and as Chutney objected, I saw a sort of froth drop off one of his eyeteeth,

'On me,' he said.

'Hear that?' I asked Frank.

'I heard it,' Frank smiled, and he made the drinks and Chutney paid, and turning to me Chutney put his hand on my arm, smiled shyly, and asked me where I had heard that? and I said I hadn't heard it (I had), I simply knew it

(I did), everybody (me), knew it: that that businessman was bored and rich and secretly in love with men.

Long-of-the-tooth Chutney scowled, and whispered simply impossible.

I know, he added, for a fact it isn't true. Can't be.

I sighed, yeah, he uses his marriage for a cover, and I said, look, everybody, even those that don't, do, and those who won't only don't, and those who could would if they had a chance and it works the same in reverse, those who could would and probably will, and it works the same with women, and I looked Chutney in the eye, and said think back in your own life. Be honest with yourself, and I put my hand on the back of his hand, and his hand was on my wrist and he made a coy little blue smirk and chuckled well Fielding, if you can't go New York Central, go Pennsylvania, and I heard Amelia laughing, as if above me.

I looked at the Illinois landscape below me, and banked the Cub in sweeping left and right horizontal curves, and then I did hammerheads, he wouldn't do a loop, and then he brought the plane down, and landed and taxied up to the hangar where she waited, knowing what I had known too, in the sky, taking Missouri rain showers together, and in New York soaping and rinsing each other in an original tactile entelechy and afterwards dried our bodies, and she sprinkled me as she did herself, with baby powder laughing Yes, dear, as I said I smell like Mommy.

We were using each other's words, really personifying each other through language, and when I'd say shit Philip could laugh and fake a face, and say oh *wow*, and I learned how to vanish and appear, yet not with the style they had. We learned our differences, too. When to leave each other alone. And I learned to handle her rare but savage reactions to her tragic past, so when we fought I let her go to the edge of her vision of her past, for her release, but never beyond to hurt her. She once said I was hot for her sister, whom I hadn't met, and who had slept with Amelia's husband, and I said only insofar as I love my own sister there's a residue of sex—forget it. But she didn't forget it, and was cruel only in her silences, and I cruel in my angry impatience over small things which I fought to control, and with her conscious power she helped me by speaking direct, and so I spoke direct too. I was glad my extension of her was male because she could redirect my impatient and self-conscious energies. I was physically stronger than she was so could physically help and protect her even from herself with my consciousness, we established true dialogue, and I was glad her extension of me was female, for the creative birth potential we needed. We were creative people, and had good ground for the future. Distance crystallized and stretched out within us, to where? Through us to the past, and thence the future.

Philip and I watched the All-Star game (and later the Series), and one afternoon, rather late, just before they went to England, as I was ploughing through Ishmael Reed's wild first novel, Philip kind of sidled up to me and said,

'Fielding?'

I smiled.

He smiled. He said let's go out and play some ball.

I told Amelia, and Philip got the bat, ball and his glove, and as we headed out to the park by the river, she said,

'Don't be late for supper.'

She laughed: *Is that in our book?*

It sure is

She raised an eyebrow, parted her lips and looked at me: 'Will you show it to me?'

I nodded, and Philip tugged at my elbow.

Come on shit

'The storyline,' she smiled. I heard her telepathic laughter and I said, 'is us,' and tossed her a worldwide wink, and said along with my movie-star smile:

'No. We won't be late.'

Champagne for Everybody—
This One's on God

143

The loss was so unhappy the whole team was angry, and on edge. I had pitched the worst game in my life, and—Joe took me out in the top of the third, and as I went off the field in that special sickening anger I knew if we lost—and this was the championship game—it would be because of me, and we did lose and it was because of me.

I didn't have anything, and when I was able to get my fastball over it went in four inches above the knees, Tommy kept yelling at me to keep it down, and I couldn't, and I got wild and filled the bases on walks and threw a neat fastball—four inches above the knees to their shortstop, who was a hostile bastard, and who hit it down the left-field line for a double. Three runs scored, and they were laughing at us.

So, at the end of the inning, finally, I sat in the stands in Central Park and looked at the skyline and thought all the immortal things great losing pitchers think.

Chicky relieved and did beautifully, but we made two infield errors, our left fielder misjudged a fly and it got by him, and our right fielder held the ball too long after a catch in the sixth and a run scored, and we were down ten to four.

Their pitcher was good, and a very pretty narcissist, with baby fat and big feet, and the kind of shady eyes of city kids who faintly resemble country kids who can't express emotion. He had a good curve, and he got me out on a changeup good, but that day I was nothing anyway, forever angry and I guessed with a sigh, it was that I had been drinking too heavily the night before and it had all ended up depressing. I tilted toward chaos again, Amelia and Philip were flying to England, and the magazine just out with my great story. The art director did a good layout job and with the illustration of the Kat it really looked swell on the page, but I worried and moped, telling myself she'd be back, she and I had made it, and in her absence were as together as one as always, in the odd incest of love, she was so much me, and I her, I repeated and repeated to myself that love crystallizes past and future: *her remarking the storyline is the field of energy*, but on the pitching mound I was unreal to it—this softball world of guys and fun—and I, everybody, I was such a sucker for myself. I couldn't concentrate on Tommy's glove, he was a great catcher, and knew me, my eyes searched the sky, Amelia was in the air heading for London, and dimly I thought, can she see me like my airplane-pilot sister could? Sadly, I grinned: the little prince pitched miserably.

I felt like my own third person, my own fall guy. Was I the other? Was I? Shadows. Fog. I was apart, and she left my field to fly to London, I was alone, and after all the years, The Everybody Years, of old and new, of separations in love, of death of my father, here we were, here I was, separated again, and I fell into the loneliness of single self in sudden horror, as when the superficial becomes actualized, and then critical, crucial, *I couldn't find an-other to be*, stunned and shaking and Tommy was yelling at me to get the ball in, smacking his glove, and I thought as I glared in trying to concentrate on the center of Tommy's glove, my target, it had to work, though she was gone we were of each other, and I licked my lips as Tommy shouted, and I went into my motion: ball three.

Then I was walking off the field with Joe at my side. Chicky came in and got them out, and we were at bat and suddenly there were two outs. Tommy went into the batter's box, I was coaching on first, and I didn't hear what Tommy said to their pitcher. I saw Tom—then I saw their pitcher come off the mound toward Tom, while rubbing the ball in his hands. He said something to Tom, and Tom lowered the bat and took a couple of steps toward the pitcher, the umpire came around to talk to Tom, but then turned, and ran back behind Warren Finnerty (their catcher), and a couple of guys on both benches stood up. Tommy laughed, and spoke again to their pitcher who looked at Tommy. I saw Tom point at his own chest and I knew Tom, Tom was grinning, and I saw him standing there and I thought, well, well, a fight? Tommy is angry too, and I smiled warmly and their pitcher glowered a little, kicked up a puff of dirt, turned abruptly, and went back to the mound and began to pitch to Tommy. He walked him. When Tom was on first base laughing with me he turned, and yelled at their pitcher: HEY MOTHER FUCKER, LOSE YOUR STUFF?

A guy on our bench yelled WHAT STUFF and I realized—our whole team was angry, and my eyes brightened. Boy, I was too, and I went over to our bench to take a nip of the vodka Roberto and I were sharing, when Charley Lowery gestured to me from up in the stands, so I went over and he grinned and his face got red as he laughed, and Mimi was laughing Fee, this'll do you, and he poured me something in the cap of a thermos, and handed it down over people's heads and I drank it, ice-cold vodka mixed with ice-cold beef bouillon and herbs and wow, *boy* —I, it was I was Ronald Colman, rediscovery of Shangri-La, God it was so *good*, and I felt so much better, but Charley I said, for the love of Jesus and Joe DiMaggio, why didn't you give this to me when I was, I gestured to the pitcher's mound, out there?

You know, I shoulda, Charley said. The biography of Charley Lowery—just kidding Charley.

He gave me another slug, and I drank it and felt so immediately of excellent health that I went to the backstop, against which Joe gloomily leaned, and I said gaily we're going to beat these creeps.

Mike drilled a line drive into center and their short fielder made a diving catch, and the inning was over. Tommy was going into third, because he had gotten a good break on the pitch.

He would have scored, and Joe said, We are?

It happened fast. In the seventh we scored two runs, Wells walked and the bases were loaded and there was one out. The other team was frantic, and their star, young babyfat, was as nervous as a jumpy junkie, and as Cousin Eddy picked up a bat, an old woman dressed in black limped out of the bushes behind the stands and crept along the first-base line toward right field, and Jerry Houk yelled from our bench BETTER SHAPE UP COCK SUCKER, YOUR MOTHER'S WALKIN' OUT

Everybody laughed and their pitcher blushed and gnashed his teeth and threw around a few dirty looks, and we clapped and cheered and Cousin Eddy smacked a thunderbolt between short and third, but their shortstop had intuitively broken with the pitch, got the hard hop, threw home, one, and Warren went to first for the double play, they were out of the inning, the score was ten to six and we were stunned. Joe put his fist against his forehead, and snarled how did that guy *get* there.

Our team was in shock, and furious: Cousin Eddy had really belted that ball, and their pitcher sat on their bench grinning because he knew we were through, and he'd been lucky.

So what did we do?

We swung for the fences, and left men on base in the eighth and didn't score, and in the ninth, two out, the score ten to six and nobody on base Tommy was at bat and he swung for the fence on the first pitch and missed and it was strike one. So it was over.

He took two balls, and on the next one swung for the fence and missed and it was two and two and he stepped out of the batter's box trying to grind the bat handle into sawdust he was so angry, the pitcher was almost laughing, the smug son of a bitch, everybody see his arms around hisself and his kissing hisself and not even enjoying it, and I stepped toward Tommy and said

'Ponzio, this winter—remember me and a three-letter word: H-I-T.'

Tommy laughed. He had had a bad year at bat, and here it was the last inning of the last game, the *big* one, and we were losing and we coulda beat those bums, and Tommy and I looked in each other's eyes for a second and suddenly in my heart I knew, and I knew Joe knew also in his heart, and I felt the knowing in our team, Gold, and Bruce, Bob, José, Larry, Mike, Eddy, Wells, Blackie and Henry and it was an everybody voice saying to Tommy, *do it*, and—

Under that blue city sky with a skyscraper horizon, there was Tommy, stepping into the batter's box, gripping the bat, high on its angle, his elbows up in the aggressive stance, in blue-denim bellbottoms, and the crisp white T-shirt with our team's name across his chest in the sudden spectacle of crystallization of blood and fire, that we were all suddenly imbued in the wood in Tommy's hands, that we were the spirit and the grain, and Tommy was—the Other in us all—and especially me, as the pitch came in and the elements went to work, the ball broke too soon, came in on the letters and Tommy stepped into it bat whipping and ripped it on a line a foot above the leaping shortstop's outstretched glove, as Tommy dug into and was then around first base and leaned toward second, and the ball rose into the far-distant fields of deep left center where nobody was as Tommy came around second and angled toward third, eyes blazing, and we were all on our feet cheering as he took that long heroic and racy turn into third to make the straight run into home, and we yelled the more as the pitcher came in to back up the catcher, their centerfielder finally found the ball, made a throw to their shortstop somebody ought to write a book about, and the shortstop turned—hesitated—and threw, the catcher Finnerty stumbled, the pitcher came forward straddling home plate, and in a blur it was Tommy coming into home black eyes burning fiery and face chalked with violence, his running body turned, shoulder dipping for the impact with the pitcher's body, and the pitcher's face was white in terror waiting for the throw to come to him—

We cheered, we laughed, we threw our hats and danced and waved our hands as the throw went wild and Tommy slid in home, safe in a cloud dust angels would envy, it was so beautiful, and the last we saw of their pitcher was he was doing everything he could to get out of Tommy's way, I woulda killed him, Tommy said to me later, at the bar at Max's, if he'd a been there, and I laughed, I know, and I said, but what was it you said to him earlier? and Tommy poured some champagne into my glass, as our teammates cheerfully surrounded us, Tommy said whenever their pitcher was at bat I gave him a lot of loud lip and he got sore, so he finally said something back to me. But, I said to Tommy, I saw you speak to him when you were at bat, not when you were catching. Yes, Tommy said, didn't you see him gesture at me?

No, I said. Ah, Tom said, well that mother fucker shook his finger at me and said he was going to get me—

A ha, I said.

Yes, Tommy said, and that's when I said to him: Here I am: come: *get me*.

His black eyes flickered, and I remembered the pitcher, standing there looking at Tommy, because he didn't know what to do, because Tommy had left the decision up to him, and—what to do? What to do, when you're afraid?

Absolutely, and I tossed my head, and said loudly, Well, fuck 'em, we won.

Like a rushing wind it went, sweeping down the length of the bar in dizzying laughter, in delight, and in release, we yelled WE WON, and we drank champagne, and we got drunk, we all got drunk, and the people thought we were crazy and we were crazy, *I* was, in the found Other warmth: of Tommy, the home run, *us*, winning ourselves together, the angry spirits in the wood, Amelia, God, winning the storyline: we won! We took the long bus ride home. Afternoon's end, and I felt so close to her. I felt a tug at my elbow, *Fuck* 'em! Turning, H'RAAY, I, in disbelief expecting myself, or Philip, disengaged myself from Mike and Wells to turn and face the waitress Linda, her upturned face, as her hands held two orders of hamburgers and french fries to be delivered to that hungry couple in the front booth, and with a soft wink behind rimless glasses, she asked,

You still in love with that lady editor?

I nodded. Well, where is she? cried Linda. In flight to England, I said, and Linda laughed, well if you're ever bored, and walked away to the people as our left fielder José put his arm around my shoulders and we sipped champagne, and Bob Povlich, seated at the bar in front of me, turned to face me, said he had seen another mediocre story of mine in some faggot magazine, we all laughed, and he asked me if my new book was out, no, I said, next month, and he asked, as we laughed harder,

What's the title?

The Mandalay Dream.

What! You stole my title! That's mine, why you—

All right, take it easy—

Povlich (to bartender Richard): This guy, do you know him?

Bartender: Sure, so do you.

Povlich: Who, this fuckin' creep? Buy him a drink.

January, 1971–June, 1972
New York